The Healing Monsters

Vol. 1

Edited by

SHAWN MACOMBER & KRISCINDA LEE EVERITT

Despumation Press
Pittsburgh

Despumation Press

Published by Despumation Press, Pittsburgh, Pennsylvania in 2016.
www.despumationpress.com

ISBN 978-0-9961680-5-2

Edited by Shawn Macomber and Kriscinda Lee Everitt
Cover Photo by Wayne Massey
Cover Design and Book Layout by Anthony Everitt

For Katherine and Dustin.

Table of Contents

Introduction

Growing up, I was surrounded by boys (and two older biological sisters) that were mostly about ten years older, and coming and going to and from different foster homes and facilities. They were in and out of my life during childhood, but I always had at least two at home. The principal impact on my early development came from my brothers until they both left for the military. I had a lot of influences, a lot of teenagers coming from different backgrounds that brought with them their styles, and it was only a matter of time that one of those hit and stuck with me: Gun N' Roses.

Appetite for Destruction was my first taste of something musical I liked. My brothers listened to it heavily, and when Pantera's *Cowboys from Hell* came along, I became hooked on that. From there it was only heavier and faster, more of me in the music and less the impression by others.

In my late teens, my BMX riding started to slow down due to an, at the time, unknown illness of diarrhea accompanied by blood and vomiting, severe stabbing pain, and fainting, which would later be diagnosed as Ulcerative Colitis and bring about the removal of my large intestine. This is now thought to have been misdiagnosed by a new gastrointestinal (GI) team, whether it was Ulcerative Colitis or the Crohn's Disease in the throat and small intestine, I'm being treated for now. Bedridden, I discovered authors such as Clive Barker. Reading *The Books of Blood* not only sparked my imagination, it inspired me, and I began jotting down little pieces—flash fiction, vignettes, or if you will, "micro fiction." While hospitalized some five years later by a more competent doctor, when I had my surgeries, I found the writing a pleasant escape; I could leave my own reality and create another, build that world and its people, then destroy it all. My first submissions were from the patient communal computer on the surgical floor. My first professional sale was a story that I wrote while in a hospital bed.

Having all the issues of Inflammatory Bowel Disease (IBD) being dismissed by family, friends, bosses, general practitioners, gastrointestinal doctors and surgeons, and those who simply didn't care to listen, to be able to create a place for them to dwell in the mind and on paper, and live out their own hell, was cathartic. It was something that, although I tried, I still couldn't match that which I many times hid and smiled through, and still do.

All of us "Crohnies" have that forced smile and when you truly know us, you know when we're faking it.

Now that I have a new GI team, we have a plan and are taking it with blunt optimism. What has been the real motherfucker of it all is dealing with the insurance, waiting for them to decide if and what doctors and treatments are needed and covered. It's a real eye-opening butt-fuck that some drugs cost $1,100 for a month's supply. And it has been mentioned recently that if my first, or second, or eighth GI doctor had taken my illness seriously, I wouldn't be in this position and the Crohn's wouldn't be as severe, and neither would the bills.

Now, I've been on a year-long chemo run. And after this

bout of C-Diff, there will be my yearly colonoscopy to see if things have spread, or if my J-pouch (fake rectum) needs any retooling, touching or tightening up.

As I grow as a writer, and lengthen my stay here among those above ground, I try to get as many pages read in as many genres and, likewise, written. A fellow author once said it takes true suffering to be a writer. I don't agree 100% but I do believe it certainly helps. It's an outlet that allows those with the ability to create to do so without feeling boxed in. Although we may be at our desk or in our beds—disabled chronically or permanently—writing in a notebook or typing, in our mind, when we are on a good smooth flow, we can be a world away doing as we please in a body that is completely whole and healthy and well, through our characters that are and always will be extensions of ourselves even in the most infinitesimal ways.

There are times where the illnesse and disease make it impossible to create, but once we're back at it there are countless ideas ready to be birthed and the strongest, the most nagging, will always push its way to the front of the line after all that time starving for attention.

As I grew and embraced, and was embraced by, the local metal scene, my writing, my creations have been, and will be, influenced by hardcore, post-hardcore, punk, doom, thrash, stoner, noise—and as I type this, I listen to a shuffle of Victims' *...In Blood* and Royal Thunder's *CVI.* Concerning music and health, I must admit that when I receive my infusions, I have an old iPod loaded with mostly instrumental bands such as Red Sparowes, Isis, Pelican, and Russian Circles. It helps keep the anxiety down and the mind off of the goings-on around me, and to escape much like writing and reading.

I'm not unfamiliar with having to take a pill for nausea and listen to Cliff Burton kill it on "For Whom the Bell Tolls" in order to get out of bed on days I'd rather cuddle up with my Rottweiler, Bronson, and sleep for another ten hours. Which brings me to a memory…

An introduction to *Metal Maniacs* when I was about eighteen-years-old.

It was an issue published a few years before in August 1998 that featured Slayer. A friend of mine, who is now a respected local tattoo artist, had tattoo, heavy metal, and horror movie magazines littered throughout his room, and while listening to either Danzig or White Zombie, I came across that issue while we sat and listened to music and read magazines on his floor.

Looking back it's odd how through suffering with intestinal disease, some aspects and loves of life were, and continue to be, taken from me, while others were, and are just, beginning to lay seed and grow because of the same reasons. Though through it all the best was discovering those who share the common bond, who have a deep and personal relationship with heavy metal and dark fiction.

I ask that if you are reading this and don't know what IBD, Crohn's Disease, or Ulcerative Colitis is, please visit the *Crohn's & Colitis Foundation of America* at CCFA.org and take a few minutes to read. Most likely, you know someone with IBD and once you know something about it can, you can better understand what their days may be like. And if you don't know anyone with IBD, read on. There is some interesting shit.

(Pun intended?)

Dustin LaValley
2016

On The Virtue of Honestly Giving A Shit

I tend to think of all media as one contiguous media—art, film, fiction, music, you name it—taking a million different paths in an attempt to express what it is to be alive, and possibly understand what that means.

And anybody whose art-o-tainment isn't involved in that fundamental conversation about the actual meaning of life is probably either just a) not thinking very deeply, or b) manipulatively lying their ass off, trying to sell you something you neither want nor need.

Which is to say, I like honest artists most of all. People who give a shit about the story they're telling, the song they're singing, the images they're slinging. If you don't care, then why should I? It's a basic rule of thumb.

Speaking personally—as a guy who's spent his whole life trying to tell the truth as hard as possible—I'm more interested in where I'm going than I am in where I've been. Whatever I did, I already did that. But there's a certain fascination in retracing your steps. Seeing how this luminous dot connected with that one. Observing the macro-grid of dot-dot-dots, as the arrow of fate and intention points forward through time. And that goes almost double for all the art-o-tainers who inspired me, and made me want to personally double down at every stage of my long life's journey.

I think the heart of what we're doing here is just drawing each other maps. Showing each other where we've been, who we are, where we're going. So that if you wind up there, someday, you're not entirely out on your own. Others have stumbled into that same place and sussed out details that might come in handy later. Yours for the taking, should you choose to take note.

It's an insane undertaking. But last time I checked, so is life. Honestly, I don't remember signing on for this shit. But I'm sure that I must have. Cuz HERE I AM NOW!

That's why bullshit is my least-favorite friend. And why thought-through, felt-through genuine sincerity is the one ingredient I respond to most, in any artist and/or human being.

I was asked to write something hopefully devoid of painful bullshit to help introduce the noble gesture that is this book. If doing so helps the real-life people it's intended to help, that's all I fucking need to know.

I love the cross-cutting contiguous media framework herein. Writers as rockers. Rockers as writers. It's a super-fun experiment.

I hope the dots connect for you. That's what they're there for.

That's why we do this.

Yer pal in the trenches,
Skipp

Imperator-Terror Lizard (Part One)

Larissa Glasser

01

I had to admit—the beast was pretty fucking impressive, almost gratuitously epic. Even from way up in the observation deck, I could appreciate the menace of our creation: its panels, folds, scales, frills, claws, and even its color scheme—a mixture of purples, greys, and greens—conveyed power, torment, and best of all: *blasphemy*. Grathe the Usurper and his Adherent sect were going to *love* that. And once brought to their knees, we would reward their treachery with mechanized dura-steel. Then the coronation of Empress Laelea would proceed as originally ordained, and we would reclaim Maadra.

That had been the *original* plan, anyway.

Meredith Magnuson, Data Sciences Coordinator and Tactical Logistician.

I liked the sound of that. Such titles, when spoken aloud, however vacuous considering our quality-of-living predicament, gave me no small gratification—they braced me against the cold winds of my past mistakes and embarrassments. I still carried the albatross of my failure to prevent Grathe's treason. And I was supposed to have the "Gift of Context," as Empress Laelea had indicated.

"The fuck does *that* mean?" I remember asking her.

"You've got the Aelix," she told me as we cowered by a fire on the first night of the exile. "You hold the annals of the world, literally in the palm of your hand."

I shrugged. "Data isn't flesh. It stretches way further back than anything we are capable of."

"But you know how to use that data, how to *apply* it to an immediate situation. I don't."

She asked me if I'd help her learn. I told her I would. I felt I owed it to her, but didn't tell her that at the time.

Funny how the so-called "Gift of Context" may only apply when you're traipsing through the wilderness of hindsight.

As a matter of course, I ranked second only to the Empress, along with head technician Gilberto Inez and Commander Armand Trent, the leader of our burgeoning armed forces and the designer/pilot of the *Almagest*, a massive airship he'd made capable of both electro-acoustic-pulse (EAP) and sound-steam-and-storm (SSS) warfare. Along with our regent, Trent was the one to follow—he'd make it happen.

My role thus expanded, I mined millennia of data from Aelix and fed my scientific wing the ancient genetic codes of dinosauria, descriptions of massive cryptids featured in mythology and folktales and latter twentieth-century Kaijū, and for added panache—fever-dream excerpts from the journals of serial killers.

The Great Hangar of Ys measured about 1000 yards in circumference. We'd had many outages in the lab and elsewhere because we'd diverted so much energy to the arena where the lizard lay dormant. The propagation period had lasted barely a month, and finally there it was, a reality at last.

As we toiled, sequoia-sized and tireless pistons of the refinery thundered and clanged throughout the waning day. Their violent impacts exuded gong-like resonance, but after a while we got into its variable rhythms and could find ways to apply it to our work. As we researched and experimented with the genetic helix, we listened to a lot of classical-mode Slayer (nothing past ante-date 1990). Gilberto Inez, stationed beside me, kept obsessing over the taxonomic integrity of our assigned *Lacerta terrorem.* My whole staff had been debating somewhat laughable minutiae the last few days: was this thing supposed to be classed as lizard, serpent, or supercroc? We'd combined genetic patterns from the infraclass Lepidosauromorpha, but overall, we'd favored the lizard over all other taxa; we wanted the beast to *stride* and stomp rather than slither as it led the assault into the valley of Maadra.

No matter—we had still focused upon the class Reptilia because we knew of that race fear held by the Adherents. There were many things they feared, it was no great challenge to find something nearby, or within oneself.

Grathe the Usurper feared matriarchy, that was for shit-sure.

And yet, now that we'd reached this zenith of the preparations for battle, I remember feeling increasingly uneasy. I couldn't pinpoint the source of that blind spot at the time. We'd had crazy power requirements and scattered outages were common. I worried about the integrity of the data in the womb of Aelix.

Also, I realized Empress Laelea had not turned up for this great unveiling of the monster. As the lab flickered unevenly, my kidneys felt like they were undergoing similar shakes—an early symptom of the desert-borne Writhing Plague. Reports had come in that a new strain had taken hold in Ys. I hoped I could tell the Empress before we lost our ground forces to that scourge. I needed a stiff drink, and to get on with whatever ceremony was supposed to happen.

Jen and our son Daniel hadn't seen me for about sixty-two hours, and as the afternoon slumped, I finally allowed myself to contact them.

My wife didn't look at all sick when she answered.

"When was the last time you slept?" was her first question, her brow crinkled in a mock gesture of reproach.

"I look that bad, huh?"

"No, but you look about ready for a ball game."

I shifted my lenses out and rubbed a telltale eye.

"Yeah." I tried to start slowly, as a bearer of sober news ought to. "Look, I know we've been tense enough with the serpent-watch, but I've been getting reports of infantry hitting the sick wards. We think it's the Writhing, again."

She looked down, and told me she knew.

"I have to wait for the Empress to show up for whatever this big unveiling is supposed to be," I said. "Do you and Daniel have enough of what you need?"

"If by that you mean food, water, heat, shelter, security, and cartoons then yeah," she shrugged. "Otherwise we're fucked."

And still, I couldn't look away. The combination of data harvesting, propagation from far-flung and dubious genetic samples, and the necromantic sorcery of Empress Laelea had culminated in the manufacture of a fleshy war-weapon such as the world had never seen. I gripped the cold safety railing, and leaned closer to the deck window.

Under the steady blue-green glare of the crudes, the sleeping monster had *curled* in on itself because there was no longer adequate space to contain it at full stretch. It didn't seem all that displeased—actually it seemed to having beautiful dreams of overtaking the Great Walls of Maadra and snacking on the colon of Grathe the Usurper. We'd implanted such sublime thought patterns during the whelping stages, but I wondered if it would then want *us* for dessert after raging through its directives.

Its massive tail wielded a bulbous club at its end, inspired partly by the affinity of Empress Laelea for ancient *Euoplocephalus*. Far, *far* opposite, the three heads of the beast—fearsome and ugly crocodilian-shaped extremities that terminated sharply from a trinity of long, glistening, serpentine necks—rested one atop the other from east to west, close as brother triplets nesting in a cradle, constrained to that fused and depraved body.

02

We didn't know who had abandoned Ys, nor why. Of more immediate importance was that it was *there*, a cold and barely utilitarian haven of intersecting pipelines, networked platforms, and best of all, reinforced and insulated lofts that served as apartments or workspaces. Following our expulsion by Grathe from Maadra, we barely escaped the Sundered Waste, that horrid salt desert chasm-pitted by earthquakes and blazing winds. The Usurper had *meant* for us to die a physical, spiritual, social, and cultural death. In Maadra, we'd been raised in a storied and ancient culture of marble, adamant, and porphyry with green-soft trees and fountain-rich courtyards, literature and wine served readily and copiously under the blood-red sun, well connected with sophisticated traders gliding along the adjacent River Möhr.

Ys actually looked pretty awesome, considering, even from afar in the Waste—the infrastructure, tall and sharp as a mighty cluster of icicles inverted skyward, had been built *inside* the skeleton of a massive Sauropod that must have measured at least a kilometer from end to end.

We certainly couldn't linger out in the Waste. The crimson radioactivity of the desert was killing us en masse. The Writhing Plague was a terrible process of organic wasting, muscle spasms, and gangrene of the extremities. Then the Ophidians—subterranean, serpentine, fanged humanoids who found our creamy nougat especially tasty—had hampered our desperate hunting and gathering. They stood at an average of six feet tall, their scales hued either black or dark green, some of the seemingly higher rank wore elaborate geometric patterns while others were about as ornate as fen-snakes. Worst of all were their eyes—they glowed with a piercing white that you could see at night as they encircled us at a mocking distance on the jagged plains. Some even had rattlers, which were especially terrible because they knew how to appeal to our night fears with both sight and sound.

The Ophidians also took human slaves, whom they either worked to death in the labyrinthine tunnels beneath the Waste, or farmed for breeding fresh meals. As a former child slave in Maadra, that made me hate them all the more.

The day after we powered the refinery, Empress Laelea cast a boundary spell that shrouded Ys from any further incursions by the serpent-men. I'd seen them try to harry us on the very next night, and as the Empress used her Healing Magick to convalesce the writhing multitude, it was gratifying for me to watch the Ophidians being reduced to snake fricassee as they tried to muscle their way past the refinery borders. It comes full circle, fuckers.

Yet I knew we had no intention of staying there. Even as we began to adjust to a barely satisfactory existence, we all rallied behind the Empress in divining plans for the reconquest of our homeland. And as she resumed her studies into Aelix's archive of both black and white sorcery, her skills increased, as did our resolve to wreak reptilian vengeance upon Grathe the Usurper.

03

Here was a drawback: we'd not managed to grow wings upon the creature—they'd terminated at unspectacular nubs that protruded from its massive shoulders. We knew Maadra needed to be attacked from the landward side, but an aerial strategy against the city would have been satisfyingly overwhelming. Grathe was to be defeated *spiritually* as well as logistically. The Adherents *hated* flight—it stood contrary to their crippled values. Give tradition any pass, because dead-penis obsolescence is never wrong.

I stood rigid at the lab window, my hands clasped behind my back, and thought along a reverse track: had we actually overreached ourselves in a big way? Despite our own shivering limbs and growling bellies, that monster would *not stop growing*, and we were running out of world for it. Was it feeding off of something we couldn't quite see?

Calm yourself—such thoughts can be construed as treason, I remembered, and glanced furtively at the five boiled, jawless skulls, each fastened to the tops of inverted crucifixes that ringed the outcroppings of the Great Hangar in a concentric arc. Empress Laelea had placed them there. She'd told me each had been proven as a spy sent by Maadra. Although this severity seemed a new trait for her, the explanation seemed plausible enough—our greenhouses had been sabotaged more than once by Grathe's agents.

The Sundered Waste was darkening, gathering new malignity to itself. It would be night soon, and the desert would puke up the vigilant patrols of the serpent-men, whose eyes would gleam up at us hungrily as we cowered in the cold steel of Ys.

There was a metallic taste in my mouth, and I felt a newly pervasive fear of being shut out, somehow. It was a difficult emotion to trace—but now that the entity had become a tangible reality, rather than a labile fusion of curious science and imperial sorcery, did the Empress even need me anymore?

Yes, there was our accomplishment—that despite our outmoded facilities and technology, we'd created an entity specifically designed for siege warfare. And yet all that time I examined our demonic Saurian, I'd been quietly consulting my own dataset in a sort of blind and loopy kernel panic, desperate for a clue as to the cause of my growing apprehension.

I kept coming up short.

04

That previous Sunday had been the last time we would all see each other alive—in the briefing room of the North Conclave at Ys. The planning for the attack had reached its final stage, but increasing reports of spreading and resurgent Writhing Plague were a cause for major concern. No one else in the meeting had yet addressed the issue, so that worried *me.*

Commander Armand Trent stood at the head of the display, with Gilberto and I at either side. Trent had been a military legend in Maadra, one who actually encouraged conscription in a culture that had grown avaricious and soft. Grathe the Usurper had banished him only out of fear that he wasn't a traitor fuck like himself. All the worse for his righteous crusade, I mused.

Empress Laelea sat at the opposite end of the table. She looked weary, her eyes sunken, her skin very pale. Her headdress concealed most of her black hair, but I could see streaks of gray at the ends. Her pendant, a fist-sized emerald cut and cast far beyond the River Möhr, glowed very weakly. That was also her interface with Aelix, so I had to wonder if my library was also experiencing difficulty—I *churned* that fear constantly and maternally. I was also worried for Empress Laelea, of course. Our military preparations depended so much on her leadership. I'd previously tried to glean information from her sentries, but they'd not responded with anything but stoic grunts.

I had continually stipulated the limits of my advisory role to Commander Trent, but even then it was becoming increasingly clear that those boundaries were bleeding. A lot.

The Commander tapped the display screen, and its bright vector unveiled the *Almagest.* I'd never before seen an actual, full-scale zeppelin model. I'd heard these aircraft briefly outlined in The Chronicles of the Late-Green Epoch, but electro-acoustic-pulse (EAP) and sound-steam-and-storm (SSS) weaponry had rendered them somewhat obsolete. But Trent had managed to combine old and new into the *Almagest*, and that fucking ruled for me.

The ship was also designed to be a leash, a sort of steering device for the beast, controlled by our airship via dura-steel tethers, and also by Empress Laelea in a reinforced harness positioned before the creature's main frill.

The display zoomed to the schematics of the main cockpit.

"Magnuson," he began. "You'll be stationed adjacent to me. I'll be steering, but your role will be crucial the entire time. I need a constant two-way feed from you, and we need Aelix to keep the ground forces aligned with our tanks and the tactical sequence. We can't miss a single beat. Yours will be a very busy job, especially during final approach into the valley.

"Magnuson and I sit at the main deck," Trent continued. "But Gilberto, your role is also crucial."

He indicated the lower deck where Gilberto would be seated with the rest of my staff.

"Magnuson is going to need you to assist with assigning directives throughout the mainframe. We're playing with a great deal of firepower, and all it takes is a small miscalculation for the assault to buckle. Friendly-fire could ensue, and that could cause a chain reaction. Not good."

Gilberto nodded. He knew what was at stake here.

Trent went on to outline our ground capabilities. Five Centurion tank units on either side of the Empress riding the great lizard, eight dune buggies each mounted with twin EAP cannons, and about 500 ground infantry with hybrid laser-crossbows.

I adjusted my lenses and re-examined the artillery plan.

"Questions, Magnuson?"

"*Sir.*"

I stood up, and that seemed to attract the attention of the Empress. Her pendant looked like a dying green star, and she looked *emaciated*, but I had to say my piece. She wasn't the only one not feeling well that day.

"There are increasing reports of the Writhing Plague resurgent throughout the refinery. I don't see how we're going to amass our ground forces when half of them are bedridden. Or *dying.*"

I collected myself. I could feel their eyes upon me. The Empress glowered, as if to wither my noncompliance—but we *had* to address the insurgent virus, although I wanted to get the whole siege over with.

I turned to face her directly. "We need new convalescence, Empress. Please, use your Healing Magick again. Aelix reports 200 infantry sick as of a few seconds ago, and that's a conservative report. *Please*, your grace. I'll help."

Her eyes narrowed, and I felt a wave crash. It hurt, and my kidneys reacted.

"Don't you *remember*?"

She looked down, and never answered me.

Would she ever heal me? I wondered, right then. *Or would she leave me to die? Does she even need me anymore, now that she's got her daemon?* Sometimes when you start to lose a friend, you don't see what's happening until it's too late for either of you.

"I've received the same reports," she said, hoarsely. The

voice, once commanding and implacable, sounded like gravel being shaken in a can. "It is not the Writhing. It is a common flu."

Moments passed. Trent didn't try to take over, because we all knew she wasn't quite finished.

"At worst, it means we delay a week or two," she continued. "It will give us more time to collect firepower."

I remained standing.

"*Sit down*, Meredith," she said softly, with her eyes closed. She still addressed me by my first name, a habit from our contemporaneous upbringing.

I sat.

She resumed.

"What is the progress with our steed?"

Gilberto chimed in. "We're in the green," he said. *I wanted to laugh at his choice of words.* "We'll be ready to show it to you before the end of the week. The beast has never existed before, at least not that we know of. But so far we can class it *Lacerta terrorem*."

Gil, I remember thinking, *shut the fuck up about your nomenclatural fetish. Think she gives a shit? What she just heard from you was a random string of words.*

Then, Empress Laelea darted up. I swiveled back in my chair, surprised but also confused by her sudden infusion of strength.

"No," she said. "*No class.*"

Trent, Gilberto, and I glanced at one another, wondering if we were seeing an apparition instead of the Empress Laelea.

"***Imperator***," she announced as twin dribbles of blood came from both sides of her mouth. She licked at them and smiled red. "Lizard of ***Terror***. Power above all."

At the opposite end of Ys, the ecstatic purring of the beast shook the walls and lent a new, special dread to our inevitable victory.

05

Sometimes you only have to look away for just a moment for something to go terribly wrong. The best disasters are noticed only after they are too late to prevent. And this is how our own reversal attacked me from all fronts.

I once again tried to reach Empress Laelea with no success, and had no way of knowing if she had weakened still further, or if she had contracted the *common flu*, as she had called it at the military briefing. She'd proved immune to the Writhing Plague during the first healing, but I knew viruses have a way of mutating and sneaking into the dancehall.

After an all-too-brief check-in with my son, Daniel, I happened upon the observatory window facing the night-darkened Waste, and saw many more Ophidians had gathered along a nearby ridge, their eyes arrayed in a disturbingly neat formation. I stared back at them, trying to look defiant, but when the upper-serpents recognized me they began to rattle with delight and I began to heave.

I ran a quick diagnosis of the repulsion border and everything checked out. But the sudden terror still had me in full panic mode. I had stopped denying danger. Never another Grathe.

I sprang to check Aelix and found her far from idle. Her response time had slowed to an almost primordial crawl, as if some outside force had blocked my link. I'd never experienced such a delay since I'd installed her. Someone was in the mainframe, either inputting a mass of data or taking it out, the latter of which I'd thought only myself capable. That was my protection all along.

I turned to Gilberto and asked, "Are you still researching the nomenclature databank for that monster?"

He nodded without looking up—he seemed very pensive. The partition in question was going wild with data input. I asked Gilberto to type a random string of characters and save them into any primary Aelix directory. Then he did look up, as if I was fucking with him.

"Do it!" I screamed. "Quickly!"

His face widened then waned, then he wheeled back to his terminal, typed the letters and saved them. The activity registered faintly in a partition far opposite the massive data riot.

"We've got to go offline!"

My head raced with the implications of Maadra attacking us from within before we could even finish our own preparations, and by means of a device they'd once tried to destroy.

I remember my terror became overwhelmed by sadness, then anger, then a sort of spiritual paralysis I'd not felt since the night of the coup. I defied the onslaught, remembered my charge, railed against the flood, and then tapped a quick and uncorrupted sequence into my right palm.

The deck fell into complete darkness, as did my mind. A mild nausea enveloped me, and then subsided just as suddenly when a tiny white speck—a vestigial atom—slowly bloomed into the center of my periphery. The light was faint and wan, but grew in mass and luminosity as it approached me carefully. Again, I couldn't look away, but my fear was tiring out.

The object became an iris whose darkness encircled by her lambent ring looked deeper than the surrounding pitch. Sound was minimal—muffled and cottony. But I knew I wasn't dying, nor was Aelix. We were just beginning again, regrouping at both 0 and the Apocalypse, taking a pilgrimage into a nothingness whose only danger was capitulation to self-hatred and acceptance of cruel fate. My whole life, I'd kept all of my fear and doubt at an impossible balance with my opposing faith and conviction. I'd always had to let one extreme or the other determine my actions, and when I found myself at a resulting disadvantage, no later achievement could salve my mind.

I wasn't asking for the moon. I'd just wanted to survive in that freezing cold wasteland, and keep the Empress, my family, and Aelix safe from the encroachment of the leech. The Usurper and his primps did not belong in the house we'd toiled to build. *We* were the holy ones all along.

I sensed my turmoil developing into anger and indignation, because emotions of the human personality die hard. But right then, perhaps sensing my suddenly defiant turn of mind, the light before me began to take a new color, more of an earthen verdigris than heavenly white. The intensity of the light wavered, very slightly at first, then developed a more pronounced pulsing, slow and steady, as if cooing. Then the darkness of its center suddenly exploded open and overtook me.

I saw my arrest on the night of the coup in Maadra.

I saw Grathe the Usurper gather back, strike me across the face, and send me flying into a flaming pile of books. Empress Laelea, bruised, gagged, and fastened in heavy chains to the foot of her throne, seethed from behind the treasonous bigot as her eyes, red and running the kohl down her cheeks, met with mine.

And Grathe's Adherents invoked their pig-fucking god.

I saw Jen and Daniel enslaved and toiling in a deep underground mine, their backs made the consistency of cereal by lash wounds.

I saw Commander Trent go down in the *Almagest*, caught in a storm of fire and defeat.

I saw a touch-screen interface of the Aelix mainframe being tested and poked by scaled, squamate claws—

Then I saw the Imperator awaken, and turn toward me, its trio of crocodilian faces peckish, its six eyes adoring. I'd somehow wound up standing at the ground level of the Great Hangar, alone and frozen in place. The crudes were too bright—they revealed nothing but that tormentor I'd helped create. The three heads snaked toward me and screamed in unison with a hybrid voice of sub-bass frequencies, salted gravel, and demonic profanity. Despite the force of the air rush, the heat of its breath, and overwhelming volume, I still couldn't move. Its huge tail hit the opposite wall, denting the dura-steel, and resounding vibrations of the impact spread to the large window of the observation deck and shattered it outward. Glass fell all about the monster and it seemed bemused. Then came the flaming jets of acid.

That was when I flinched—I cowered, crouched, and held my head as the Imperator spat a triple stream of burning, wandering destruction all around me. I didn't know why or how the fire missed me, but I saw the bright streaks melting and pitting the walls, and soon rivers of molten detritus formed a steaming pond beneath the monster, pleasing it further. It finally drew back, folded its oversized limbs into themselves to allow more room, and regarded me with a possessed veneer of serenity.

Frantic but still too afraid to provoke a fresh volley from

the thing, I tapped my right palm, and Aelix signaled back. She said she was fine, the restart had taken care of some scattered fragmentation, but no bad or corrupt sectors had been detected in the process. Then I realized with horror why she thought she was truly intact, truly aggregate, no data missing. She no longer had the capacity nor the need to differentiate human data from Ophidian data.

The breach hadn't been caused by Grathe, after all. The Usurper, as we would see later with some small satisfaction, couldn't tell his dick from his ass, much less be able to hack into Aelix.

The Imperator burped lazily, and again the arena convulsed.

Then the laughter began, distant and then with raising intensity as it drew nearer, resonate through the scarred but still massive Great Hangar of Ys.

Empress Laelea's voice filled the air:

"*Imperator—Lizard of Terror!*

You are ready for our charge.

We made you an abomination for the sake of natural order, because nature needs something to contradict.

You thirst for the blood of our enemies, you hunger for dread.

You are a destroyer of life, and larger you will grow, still, because you will never fill the world with enough loathing and hate.

Imperator—Lizard of Terror!

We will boil their skulls, and brand their corpses with your standard."

The doors flew open and Empress Laelea entered the arena, flanked by a veritable entourage of highborn Ophidians, their white eyes glowing but trying hard to adjust the intensity of the crudes. Her skin had turned from sickly white to a subtle blue-green, her bloodshot eyes now a jaundiced yellow with leaner, black-slitted pupils, and her black mane of hair writhed about as if by a disembodied, self-contained breeze. Her pendant glowed like an emerald sun, more brilliantly than it ever had during her most extended reveries of healing our sick. In her manicured hands she carried the decapitated, shorn head of Commander Trent, its eyes gouged out and lower jaw removed. It looked more like a flaccid jellyfish than anything that had once been heroic or human.

Holy fucking shit, I remember thinking.

"I have brought the sixth traitor's skull," she hissed. A spasm of controlled giggles rose from among her new serpent-allies. One of them carried a freshly-minted inverted cross.

Right away, I drew my service pistol and aimed it at the group. Of course, I targeted far wide of the Empress. I actually recognized *Aspnath*, a highborn Ophidian ambassador who had once tried to trick us into powering down the protective border of Ys. I told him he should first hand over our citizens being worked to death in their tunnels, or if that preliminary didn't work for him, to go fuck his egg-laying mother. The ambassador recognized then the same look in my eyes that I'd given him during that first fruitful negotiation, and the hood of his cobra-head widened as he drew back.

"Meredith!" shouted the Empress. "Holster your weapon at once!"

She heard the click of the safety, then looked down at the head of our Commander in her hands, the storied soldier who was going to bring us back home, back to Maadra, or fight like hell trying.

"*Gunsss*," she hissed. "They are nothing in battle without

Ophidian Magick. *My* power protected you from the firestorm of the Imperator. You will get used to this, trust me. You remain my slave, and you will *worship* your terror."

The shock began to shear away. I lowered the gun, and my terrible *Gift of Context* deepened. I was trapped between two equal hatreds, and then two equal fears.

She smiled at me, close-lipped and with impish dimples, then turned back to the entourage, chinned toward the doors, and the serpent-men parted into halves for her revelation.

In walked Jen, our son Daniel, and Gilberto. They were each chaperoned by the sentry holding a laser-crossbow to the backs of their heads. At that advanced stage of what I'd thought had been the Writhing Plague, each sentinel had gone through similar physical and spiritual changes as the Empress. This had indeed been a new strain, not fatal but *transformative.* My family looked absolutely petrified, not only at the turn of events, but also at the three-headed colossus lounging about before them. Gilberto just looked dejected and exhausted.

The Imperator purred.

"*Meredithhh,*" persisted Laclea, mockingly emphasizing her metamorphosis. Her pendant pulsed with serpentine treachery. Our eyes met, with newly divergent loyalties, destinies.

"I'm promoting you General of the Assault, *Magnusonnn.*"

She grinned at me with baby fangs.

Real Mature

Andrew Bonazelli

There was only one way to go about it, and that was hardening both palms into table tennis paddles, crushing his skull with one concentrated handclap and force-feeding her the fragments with a pestle and funnel.

Actually, no, there were a lot of ways to go about it, and Redding had been through them all. For a while, there was a Top Five scribbled on the refrigerator dry erase board, which he would repeat and perfect, just to have a hobby again:

1. Plastic-wrapping her face just before she crammed her tongue down that fucking turd's throat, popping her head off like a bottle cap, swinging it around by the ponytail and caving in his chest

2. Lining the two of them up execution-style before a crossbow, lit cigarettes and candles introduced liberally to any and all conceivable orifices

3. Letting them go at it atop the quilt his grandmother knitted in the bedroom he furnished in the apartment he put

down first, last and deposit for; lobbing in a hand grenade just as they made each other cum

4. Compressing her forehead and jaw hard enough during fellatio to eliminate his manhood

5. Squeezing water-resistant fixative down her belly while he fingered her in the shower; watching them thrash around for a few seconds; sky-hooking her plugged-in blow dryer over the curtain

On occasion, Redding would test his telekinetic aptitude by squinting hard and imagining blood bubbling out of the fingernail scratches she'd left on his arms and back, slivers peeling into open gashes, reddening the skin slowly and pervasively until entrails flooded out and collapsed into a heap of gore.

These tests failed.

In his new life as an apparition, Redding's omnicidal skill set was limited strictly to the hands-on.

That he infused such grandiose detail into each exercise was peculiar. Redding had never harbored sadistic impulses as a boy, save the occasional bored front porch flyswatting. Now, every night afforded a new opportunity to concoct far more unspeakable means of amputating, excoriating, exploding, bludgeoning, or mutilating Felicia and whatever young man or woman or men and women she happened to be consorting with—the specific identity of the gentleman in the aforementioned scenarios being both variable and negligible.

Redding did not merely punch the clock. He strived to accrue overtime.

But not with relish. Redding never chortled or smacked his lips or sipped cognac or exhibited any discernibly enthusiastic emotion during these sessions—not because he was ashamed of any of it, but because he never thought to be. He wouldn't have been *opposed* to theatrical extroversion. And, sometimes, he rued that his innate impassivity dulled the spectacular righteousness of it all.

But this was fleeting.

Man's inhumanity towards man, and woman, and men and women, was not worth examination when molested by the paranormal. Rule books had long ago sailed out the window: the sessions were all that mattered, taking to hard task the woman who literally and figuratively made a ghoul of him.

The true joy of hurting, he had long ago discovered, was to tower over victim for the first time as owner.

Here in Felicia's bedroom, illuminated only by a secondhand television puttering along a thousand-channel gauntlet, Redding was reminded each and every midnight that sequels sucked. When the elated panting subsided and the blinders were sapped of crimson, all there was to do was towel off, smoke or gawk his way to stupefied inertia.

Except it wasn't that simple.

After a particularly spirited bout of, say, #1, Felicia's random paramour would, understandably, scamper around the bedroom gasping and retching. But after a minute or two, he would slow to a trot, collect his bearings, pluck her cranium out of his thoracic cavity, haul the toolbox from the closet, reattach it to her neck with masking tape and staple gun, and they'd commence frenching, disrobing, talking dirty, lapping at each other's assholes, and so on. These improvisational reupholsteries, suffice it to say, often made matters less than aesthetically (and, many times, gastrointestinally) tolerable.

Sometimes, in lieu of what Redding once regarded the

pinnacle of horror—any human besides him pawing all over his beloved Felicia—he was treated to a legless torso stump-fucking a pelvis with eyeballs for ovaries.

None of this gave Redding *that much* pause, whether it was his own design or unhappy accident.

There was a routine to attend to: beat all organic matter to gunk, gallop to his former bathroom to expunge, wash up, trudge past his L-shaped contemporary sectional couch, twin cherry armoires, and the framed Bauhaus lithograph he bought her after the breast lump was removed—he used to trace the scar around her areola with his pinkie, wishing he could erase it—gargle tap water, and return to the bedroom to find Felicia and company in perfect (enough) working order, going about their business with a ferocity and innovation that made the randiest pornographers look like fumbling virgins. The impermanence of it all did wonders for retarding the emotional pendulum. Redding would often simply sit in the corner rocker to observe and wonder how he possibly could have fucked things up so galactically that the love of his life wound up inhaling cokefreak jerk-offs, cumming like the fourth of fucking July every single time.

The once impeccably tidy boudoir had degenerated to an unflushed toilet in his absence. Felicia had taken to depositing her halter tops, jeans, tips, pills, and dirty flatware in a festering heap in front of the closet. Occasionally, by force of habit, Redding would rise from his perch to grab a tattered magazine, only to narrowly dodge her and some Eurotrash bulimic ricocheting around the room like super balls, at which point he would stumble and faceplant onto the malodorous jizz swamp of a carpet. At which point he would shoot himself in the face and make things even worse.

This was *not* habitual. Redding only killed himself three times after his original demise.

After the first, he was immediately resurrected to discover his father penniless and disfigured. After the second, he was immediately resurrected to find his penniless and disfigured father prostituting his mother for hot meals. By the third time, Redding was almost bemused by the perverse and vindictive nature of "God," and figured he'd keep doing himself in to see how macabre an impressionist the man upstairs really was.

That time, he didn't even lose consciousness, just healed right on the spot like Felicia and her fucktowels, except cleanly.

After which, she and her armada of lovers' post-coital pillow talk began to consist solely of jokes about his cock, which shrank an inch and developed bleeding sores each time he pulled the trigger on himself.

When Redding actually left the apartment, that was when things started to get disagreeable.

Years of Decay

John Edward Lawson

Daniel David studied the ink rippling under his skin as it surged in time with his muscles, while someone's fingernails carved new wounds across his old scars. The relief map of reknit tissue along his arm was nearly as faded as the tattoos telling his life story. That's because his life ended, cut short so long ago.

Almost as short as that of the man struggling in his grasp. The black clothes looked to be roughly Daniel David's size, and weather resistant as well. They would serve as excellent replacements for the current ensemble of stained, tattered rags bound to his skin by rope. The Heckler & Koch 416D, automatic Benelli M4, and Beretta 92F 9mm had run out of ammo, then come apart after being repurposed as tools over the years. The tactical vest eventually had to be cast aside because it was punctured scores of times over. The ballistic helmet was hopelessly fractured, and the Taser X26 ran out of juice years before the Motorola radio finally stopped transmitting. The last of his equipment to survive were canisters full of flex cuffs, thankfully not so biodegradable as the tree huggers would have wanted way back in the day.

Now that he stopped to consider it: why should Daniel David desire the other man's clothes? Seasons had ceased to change so long ago he could not accurately recall the passage of time. Besides, extremes of heat and cold had long stopped holding any power over his resolve.

It did not matter that the man's bladder began to empty into his trousers as the radius of Daniel David's right forearm refused to snap against his windpipe. Extremes of smell would not deter Daniel David from donning the garb. The sensations, which had filled the void since Carrie left, would break the sanity of lesser men so he shut them out.

A steel knife suddenly occupied space in Daniel David's left thigh. The metal penetrated several inches of rectus femoris and sartorius before the tip directly explored his femur. The stranger had miscalculated if he thought this pain would improve his fate. The musculature of Daniel David's face contracted as the result of some involuntary muscle memory, with the corners of his mouth turning upward while lips parted to expose his teeth. Carrie had enjoyed this aspect of his appearance, saying it was charming.

At the thought of her voice—and its lack of malice or terror or duplicity—Daniel David snapped the man's neck.

Why? Because.

Collapsed buildings leaned together forming a pyramid, their windows empty sockets. The steel and mortar and concrete had twisted into this architectural chimera after a series of blasts set by demonstrators, protesters, Occupiers and leftists and

Libertarians and white supremacists. Nobody held a monopoly on violent paranoia after the epidemic got out of control. Crowning this monument to failure is the flame. It was the fire that kept Daniel David anchored to this spot. If he failed to keep the fire going Carrie would not know where to find him, would think that he had died or was too weak willed to cut it in her absence.

He preferred to remember Carrie as she was on that one perfect day when they were at Sheriff Mahfouz's home for an evening of toasts and presentations and more food than Daniel David could hope to sample. The head of the State Sheriff's Association himself snapped a picture of Carrie embracing Daniel David in the dappled shade of a magnolia in the estate's large back yard. Their unabashed smiles revealed how utterly smitten they were with each other, and with the future.

Then the future arrived in the form of multiple extinction level events. The effects of the war had been somewhat mitigated, and there were stopgap measures for the disease, but the environmental deviations were enough to force the bulk of survivors underground. None of the spaceships hastily built by the elite had been launched due to startup sequence errors. That was the rumor, anyway.

Daniel David had originally been one of hundreds occupying the collapsed network of structures forming the pyramid. That number rapidly dwindled, until the only company he kept was that of loners who came after hearing tell of a purifying fire atop a pyramid. It was said the fire—by means of the machinery attached to it—would burn away the disease. They were violent, desperate scavengers. Where had they come from? Nobody would ever know. They were secrets to be added to the conspiracy database. He interred these secrets in the sand out back with thousands of co-conspirators.

It was the intersection of roads at the pyramid's base that made it possible for them to survive the blasted landscape and the shadowy things which now inhabited it. Only one or two found their way to him per week. The interim was Daniel David's "lean time."

Why? Because.

One day specialists had ridden in on a machine unlike any Daniel David had ever seen before. Nobody knew what to expect: was this some remnant of a military convoy? Where could they possibly be going?

"To end this, of course."

As an answer, that sounded simple enough. How could Carrie not go for that? Ending it. Weaklings always found the struggle too much to bear, and could not endure the day in/day out of it. Supposedly the population of specialists housed in the enormous and elaborate vehicle could physics themselves in and out of all sorts of different dimensional coordinates.

A knee injury had ended Daniel David's MMA career in his youth, but that did not mean he was not still a man, one honorable and capable of bringing the fuck-you-up-the-ass attitude when need be. Everyone in the camp began to look at him sideways, though, when he was not gung-ho about jumping in some strangers' contraption and abandoning the home they had built, gutting the community. The bulk of his clan were going along with the scientists in their crazy scheme to find a cure for the disease, to try and reverse the permanent darkness blanketing the Earth, and who knew what else.

Since then how many mothers had he witnessed put to death, how many children beheaded or devoured alive, how many grown men reduced to their component parts as they watched, unable to halt their own slow-motion death?

Carrie would make sense of it all. Just seeing her again. There was nothing carnal about it; his tenements of lust had been condemned ages ago, abandoned for the promise of standing in her presence just one more time with the flash blindness caused by looking directly at her, the overpressure of her voice rolling over him in waves. It would be enough to sit next to her in comfortable silence as the machines processed their blood, straining out new variants of the virus.

But they had insisted on taking her away. They had even slung some incendiary rubbish about dragging him along with them. Somebody had to stay behind to act as a shepherd, though, to maintain the distribution systems just in case they came back with the cure they sought. He was the man for that job, he insisted, because he could endure it. Just in case.

Carrie had not been able to meet his eyes in that moment, nor did she say goodbye.

When the lurkers stabbed him, burned him, or smashed his bones with lengths of metal they always looked right at him. That brief human connection was what kept him going. And the scientists, the doctors and specialists, they had said he wouldn't make it. That he would change over time.

Why? Because evil.

The fire was meant as a beacon, a rallying point, not an actual cure, but in time perception can alter reality. As more and more survivors arrived and were disposed of, Daniel David came to perceive himself as the cure. The cure to human weakness.

That subject was always one of hot debate between himself and Carrie. She was always on the move, upwardly mobile and ambitious, for which he criticized her as being stuck on a treadmill—staying in motion yet keeping everything just the same. For her part she accused him of externalizing his own problems and seeing them everywhere he looked. Ironically, she believed he lived in fear of change.

They told Daniel David if he stayed he would be gradually altered, that he would eventually succumb, but they were just afraid of seeing him strong enough to survive on his own. Staying in the resting place of their relationship caused his strength to grow exponentially.

The machinery was not responsible for his condition. His genes and willpower drove him onward. He kept the machines in top form, though, just in case. Just in case those crazy bastards did somehow make it back to the right time and place instead of getting stuck somewhere hundreds of thousands of years before the Ice Age trying to retrieve some extinct plant or another. He would do his duty and maintain the equipment just as he maintained his own physique. After all, the survivors continued to crop up in ones or twos, all of them baring weapons and hatred and inexplicable greed for the fire.

Or, perhaps not so inexplicable considering Daniel David's penchant for suggesting by means of radio there might, in fact, be a cure awaiting any who made it to the pyramid's fiery pinnacle. That was back when he actually had some hope Carrie's mission might succeed, and that her team would just phase back into the timeline without a hiccup. Those messages were meant to build a new community with which to impress Carrie on her return. He ended those broadcasts soon enough, but the damage had already been done.

And the ceaseless stream of interlopers continued to trickle in.

Why? Because evil.

The silence broke as the sounds of someone unfamiliar with the terrain attempted to surmount the pyramid. There were at least three of them. Feet slipped and dislodged bits of crumbling wall.

"Why do you even wanna see this place?"

"Yeah, is it because of the legend?"

Those two voices belonged to men, but the third member of their expedition remained silent. Daniel David did not bother moving from his perch. He had stayed motionless for the better part of a day. Or two. Or three. The thin layer of grime coating his skin suggested a lean time had passed since he troubled himself with anything. A brief test of his joints revealed he had not lost his prowess.

"She doesn't know about the legend."

"Lookit. See there? Nobody ever gets up to that fire and comes back down."

"Sure, some folks make it up there. They been seen up there. Why they never get seen again is anybody's guess."

"A certain contingent always say it cured them, so why they wanna come back? Course they don't. Them's the hopeful ones. Most folks don't believe in that foolishness. We know the real reason."

"See, there's a vampire what lives up in these here ruins."

Silence, followed by trudging, grunts, and a snicker.

"She don't believe us."

"I wouldn't either!"

"Smell that?" The group paused, hesitated, lurked in the

same spot just a little too long. "Your nose don't lie. We all done smelled death in our time, but that there smell ain't natural. It's worse than death."

Supernatural cures, supernatural curses, it was always the same with humanity's last few remnants. Daniel David and his message were irrelevant in the final equation. Their deceit was, in the end, not due to his words so much as their incessant desire to believe in something greater. Primitive intelligence is what doomed them. They were beholden to Bronze Age modes of reasoning.

They continued moving, but not before Daniel David had descended in a single fluid motion to map the weakness of the rear man's soft flesh.

Soon enough these three would be drained of their vital fluids. The machine which filtered the virus out long ago ran out of raw materials, necessitating these harvests. The weak perished so the strong might live.

Children only contained 1.75 liters of blood which, in addition to their constant need and poor cultural taste, rendered them next to useless. They served well enough to keep the lean times at bay, though.

The pair continued for half a minute before realizing something was amiss. They shifted in the darkness, calling out for their companion. Before they knew what was happening the remaining man had compound fractures of the ulna and fibula, with crushed ribs on the way. The woman turned and ran for it. She got within ten yards of the fire, and the machines surrounding it, when Daniel David's hand found her shoulder blade. She tumbled through the air, screaming in her descent, but not for long. He followed her down the pyramid's other side.

She was impaled on a strand of rebar which still had one end embedded in the pyramid's concrete. It had been meticulously sharpened for just such an opportunity, just as had all other protruding bits of metal. The face staring up at him in wonder and bewilderment was Carrie's.

That was impossible, yet the voice squeaking out broken syllables also matched his memory of her. She was begging him for help, begging him to respond. What would he say to her, anyway? Something to ease her passing, or perhaps something to make it all the more excruciating? She was the one, after all, who had forsaken him on this useless mound, left him overseer of the diseased and the dead, chronicler of unending darkness. To what gain? In the end her choices could not have possibly been worth it.

"Th-the cure . . . we found it . . . I'm the last one, baby, but I never gave up . . . knew I'd . . . I'd see you again. Here," she said, gesturing to a satchel at her side. "Inside. Take it. Put it . . . put it in the machine. Activate . . . activate the dispersal sequence and . . . and . . . and the human race can rebound. Rebuild."

Words finally failed her, so she instead smiled up at him, the first person to do so in centuries. At her continued urging he withdrew a tube full of luminescent blue liquid, framed by some unfamiliar metal alloy. After a cursory examination he figured out the locking mechanism and undid it, tossing the metal away so that he might hold the tube up to the firelight.

In his gut something was horribly awry. There was pain, or . . . fear? Yes! The sensation was so unfamiliar as to be simultaneously thrilling and enough to cut his legs out from under him. Muscles contracted, curling him into a ball, and still his paralyzed hand was unable to relinquish its grip on the tube. This thing and its contents spelled the end for him. All his power siphoned away with the push of a button.

Daniel David looked from the cure to the beatific agony of the woman he loved, and for a moment he saw exactly how to save her, how to relieve her impalement and nurse her back to health. Then the strength which had been nurtured in Carrie's absence woke and plunged the glass tube into her oral cavity. Blue liquid and shattered teeth flew everywhere, and Carrie's scream failed to compete with the sound of glass splintering in her tonsils and esophagus.

He thrust his violence into her repeatedly until she was full of bloody holes, and yet somehow she failed to succumb in the same fashion as others would. Apparently one went through certain changes whether they stayed with the smell of smoke and charred wood or went skipping all around time and space.

Would Jared be the same? He had spent years with Daniel David, far longer than Carrie had, functioning as a proxy brother. Daniel David had not grown up with siblings, so he took such close friendships seriously. Then the quest to find an uncorrupted water source had been proposed, and Jared had been the first to volunteer to leave on that suicide mission.

Contemplating this betrayal was beyond angering.

Jared had, in the end, been unable to stand the burden of daily survival as a man should, had been a lesser man whose word meant little in the final analysis, and despite this—or, perhaps because of it—Daniel David must stay vigilant over the flame to ensure it remained as his friend remembered it. Just in case . . . just in case . . . just in case . . . .

Because evil never dies.

Seven Goats: The Record Single, Side A

Mathias Jansson

The steal rudder sinks deep
Down into the black sea of vinyl
Following the maelstrom faster and faster
To the center of Hell
Scratches and notches in my speaker
Are sonar signals revealing a secret
Buried deep under the surface

By backmasking and remixing
I reveal a message forgotten since ancient time
I can hear the heartbeat of drums
The fast steady pulse of Armageddon
Guitar strings vibrating with fear
When screams of death fills the air
I hear a growling voice
A chanting voice of horror
"Ta dez un dez, ta dez un dos
Da se wez, tud ers dan

Asdez, asdez, sev got!"
Until my ears are bleeding
And my mind is balancing
On the edge of insanity

Seven Goats: The Record Single, Side B

Mathias Jansson

Tree branches are headbanging on my wall
The heavy rain patters on the Hi-Hat roof
A bass chord knocking on my door
With trembling hands I turn the record
To listen to the other side of Hell
Looking down on the dark maze of life
Hypnotizing rotating in front of my eyes
I feel I am falling deeper and deeper
Down the rabbit hole
Until I stand in a circle of stones
In the spotlight from a full moon
Seven shadows release from the dark
Dragging rusty chains in thigh leather
The red desert vibrating of thunder
From guitar, bass, and drums
When a voice from the deepest dark
Starts to sing his endless refrain of fear
"If six six six is the number of the beast

I welcome him to our feast
A new worse v~~ersion~~ is released
Seven numbers worse at least
It's too late to feel any fear
The Seven Goats are here
It's too late to pray for salvation
When Seven Goats bring damnation"

Summersault

Dutch Pearce

The plan had been so perfect: nab Priscilla, the Rices' chihuahua, leave a note of her whereabouts and how to get her back, then use the ransom money to buy a trampoline. Except who could've accounted for there being no trampolines in the Horse Trader?

They had hatched the plan the night before in their cabin. Originally an old tree stand that looked out over the strippings below, the cabin was their sanctuary from chores, parents, and the world at large. The boys had installed it, back when the ravine was still a forest, before Jimmy's dad went to jail, before Seaver's dad took off back to Texas with Marcy Minick. Using scrap lumber they stole and floated down river one night last summer from the Wolden lumberyard, the boys had first erected some walls. The roof was PVC weatherboarding that they had scavenged from the post office fire that same summer. When it rained, the sound was like the double bass on "Angel of Death."

But that night it had not rained. The air was skin-warm and sticky with the want to rain. A breeze like the gaseous emissions of a bloated carcass blew at weird intervals. And the forest surrounding their modest base was drowned in a crepuscular fugue that was only noticeable when something interrupted it, causing a deafening silence.

Seaver and DJ had cleared away the camouflaging branches and Jimmy had hobbled in ahead of them, lighting the kerosene lamp. The lamp glowed orange in the middle of the floor bringing the cabin to life with posters of warriors, women, and metal bands. Implements of ambitious destruction and petty crime were piled in every corner.

Seaver immediately went to the stack of *Penthouses* and *Playboys* he kept under a tarp pinned down by a Buddha he'd stolen from Cassandra Petrechor, the town hippie.

Jimmy pushed back a clump of greasy black hair from his eyes. The kerosene lamplight gilded his leg braces. Directing his gaze at DJ, Jimmy explained that the Rices had not actually been flying like he'd thought. DJ listened closely, his front teeth digging into his bare knee. Turns out that the Rices had gotten what was called a trampoline. As he explained what that was, Jimmy, beside the far wall, carved another scene into the wood. That night he carved a bearded man in a horse-drawn chariot throwing lightning bolts. Seaver chewed snuff he'd stolen from his Uncle Toot, spat into a Pepsi can. His attention was focused on the gooey fruit and smooth contours juxtaposed amid bearskin rugs and burning candelabra within the pages on his lap.

DJ said he would ask his parents for a trampoline for his impending eleventh birthday, but Jimmy immediately replied: "You guys don't have room for a trampoline with that horse corral. Plus your property's got a downhill grade to it. Trampoline's got to be perfectly level."

"Well, what about Seaver's yard?" DJ said. "It's flat."

"Sure," Jimmy said. "Seaver's yard'd work fine."

DJ perked up, but then Jimmy added: "But trampolines ain't cheap and Seaver's family is dirt poor."

"Screw you, Jimmy!" Seaver said, his lower lip fat with wet snuff. "Least we don't get money for being disabled."

Jimmy brushed away wood dust from his carving. He ignored Seaver, and Seaver returned to his naked women. DJ stood up and went to the window. It seemed so easy to slip through the window and sail out over the trees and away from it all.

"We'll clear out a patch," Jimmy said. "Not here, but close. First, we got to check the Horse Trader."

"Horse Trader?" Seaver said. "What for?"

DJ turned from the window, curious to hear what Jimmy was getting at.

It's said that you could find anything in the Horse Trader, Jimmy explained as he gave DJ a stack of the magazines.

Then DJ looked through issue after issue without finding a single trampoline.

"Probably still too hot of a commodity," Jimmy suggested.

If there was one in the three-month-old Trader DJ found himself hopelessly flipping through, it had long been claimed. But he looked anyway.

Then he saw it:

FOR SALE: 16 ft. rnd. trampoline, like new.
$100 OBO. (814)945-2206. 3 RD, Westover.

DJ straightened in amazement: "You guys!" He showed his friends the ad.

"Don't get your hopes up yet," Jimmy said. "The ad's months old."

"It's worth a phone call," DJ said.

"Westover's just up 226. I've made it there in less than an hour on my bike," Seaver offered without looking up.

"Yeah, but how will we pay for the trampoline?" Jimmy asked. "And how do we get it back here to the woods?"

"We can drag it!" DJ answered in earnest.

"And we're going to get money from kidnapping Priscilla," said Seaver.

Jimmy sighed. "Let's go."

DJ bolted out of the cabin and took off running up through the trees. At the bikes, before his breath even came back to him, DJ unhitched Jimmy's wagon from Seaver's ten speed and secured it to his own Huffy. He figured he would have Seaver go back to his own house to do his evening chores while he and Jimmy called about the trampoline. Seaver didn't minded feeding DJ's mom's horse after DJ showed Seaver his dad's hidden stash of Hustlers.

A screen door slapped and echoed through the quiet, empty afternoon. DJ saw Ron Livingston come out of his trailer and jog through the small patch of knee-high corn stalks to his red pick-up only to curse as if he'd forgotten something and go right back into the trailer. The screen door bounced against its aluminum frame like a dropped basketball.

"We'll have to use a payphone," DJ said to his friends as they reached him. "We can't risk a tapped line."

"What's your rush, man?" Seaver said. He had his shirt tied around his head and his BB gun was slung across his chest by a bailer-twine strap. "Jimmy's right. That trampoline's been scooped up already."

"We don't know that," DJ said. "Jimmy, tell Seaver that there's a chance it's still there."

"I don't know, Deej," Jimmy said. Seaver showed his buckteeth at DJ.

"You guys are green," DJ said. He ripped at the knot that tied Jimmy's wagon to the seat post of his Huffy. "I'm out of here." As he left, he kicked down on his right pedal to make what he'd hoped would be a dust cloud, but only sent a few pebbles rolling.

"Faggot!" Seaver shouted after DJ had rode some distance away.

DJ stepped back on his brakes and slid a 180.

"What'd you call me, Seaver?" he shouted down Ron Livingston's long dusty driveway.

"You heard me," Seaver called back.

DJ went barreling straight at him. Pedaling faster the closer he got.

Seaver threw down his sight on DJ.

DJ cranked so hard he lifted the front wheel off the ground, riding what's called a power wheelie.

Seaver fired, the sound like a whip crack. If the BB hit DJ, he didn't feel it. He stepped on the front tire, went end-o, ejected, and speared Seaver who was mid-pump for another shot. The bike tumbled after the boys. The seat caught Seaver in the face who'd somehow landed on top. Seaver rolled off DJ, holding his hand over his mouth.

Jimmy limped over to where Seaver laid kicking his legs and stifling his sobs. Jimmy pulled Seaver's hand away. DJ only stared, as Jimmy's fingers plied out Seaver's front tooth.

Seaver pushed Jimmy away and grabbed his BB gun.

He was a mess of spit, blood and dusty tears. Jimmy tried to stop him and got the butt of the Daisy right in the guts. Jimmy doubled-over, held erect by his braces. Seaver stalked over to DJ, pumping his rifle twelve, thirteen, fourteen times.

DJ remained still. He had two eyes and a whole mouth full of teeth. Seaver had just one shot, then DJ would be on him like Wolverine on Sabretooth.

Seaver aimed the barrel at DJ's right eye.

"Got any last words?" Seaver lisped through the new hole.

"Yeah," DJ said.

Ron Livingston's screen door banged again, but no one looked through the corn stalks over at the grey trailer.

"Go on then," Seaver said.

"Pull my finger," DJ said.

Seaver smirked. DJ made to stand and as he did Seaver cracked him in the mouth with the fake wood stock of the Daisy.

Sherts of one of DJ's teeth exploded in his mouth, like the time Seaver had dared him to bite a Snap Cracker.

DJ fell back to the earth, his busted lip stinging from the dirt on his hand. Above him some starlings alighted from their murmuration on a power line.

Jimmy's mom was home when the boys got back to his house, passed out in her chair. She snored and seemed to choke in her sleep. Her head looked like it was held on by her grey neck skin. She gripped a Genny pounder in her fist. A cigarette butt smoldered in the ashtray on a TV dinner-stand. Wheel of Fortune was on and Pat Sajak was bullying his guests. DJ ran his tongue over his jagged tooth. Seaver watched Vanna White.

Jimmy snuck a quarter from his mom's pocketbook and

flipped it up in the air. As it tumbled ceilingward, he said: "Heads it's still there," and on the way back down, he said: "Tails it's gone."

The coin lied. They rode down to the Countri-Mart and, with the same quarter, called the number from the ad, but no one answered. Dismayed, though still hopeful, they decided, without hanging up the phone, to ride up and check the place out.

But then DJ suddenly remembered his evening chores and rode home as fast as he could, with Seaver somewhere behind him. Jimmy stayed behind at the Countri-Mart payphone in case the trampoline people came home and answered their phone.

On his way home, DJ's dad passed him in his truck. He slowed down and rode alongside DJ as they crossed the midtown bridge. His dad pointed at his watch, shook his head, and sped off.

When DJ got home, his dad was coming out of the barn from doing DJ's chores and was already taking off his belt.

His dad had worked seventy hours that week only to come home and have to do his son's chores for him. DJ's dad asked if DJ had any idea what an outrage that was? DJ said that he did, but, to his dad, it seemed like DJ didn't know, so it was beat into him. DJ gripped the wood of the barn door and watched his father's shadow, like a primitive cartoon in the barn light. He did not weep. He was floating on the air, high above it.

At the supper table, DJ kept his head down so his parents wouldn't notice his wrecked tooth. It hurt to sit, and when his dad caught him leaning forward, he'd shove him back down into the hot pain. After dinner he did the dishes and walked out the front door. His parents were fighting in the laundry room about crust in his dad's underwear.

Seaver's mom was working the graveyard shift at the hospital. They left Seaver's little brother, Salem, in front of the TV. *Space Ghost Coast to Coast* was on.

Jimmy was asleep under the payphone. The phone had been hung up.

"Get up, man!" DJ kicked Jimmy. "You were supposed to wait for an answer. You can't do anything right!"

"Someone did answer, jizzwad!" Jimmy said. He pushed his black hair out of his eyes and hoisted himself up using the red brick front of the Countri-Mart. "Some guy that's feeding her cats answered. She's in the hospital, the lady that's getting rid of it. Story's crazy, man. Her kid died or something. Guy talked my ear off. But the trampoline's still there. Guy said we can come get it whenever."

DJ grabbed Jimmy and started bouncing up and down. Seaver fired his BB gun into the air and hooted. Jimmy shook DJ off.

"Now it's time for phase two of Operation Fearless," Jimmy said.

DJ nodded. Seaver pumped the Daisy.

"We'll reconvene at the midtown bridge tomorrow at noon. Go home and get some sleep, fellas. Tomorrow we break the law."

"How're you getting home?" DJ asked.

Jimmy pointed at the moon and let out a loud howl. DJ joined him, then Seaver. Together the three friends howled and barked at the moon and beat their chests.

The next day, DJ skipped Sunday service to watch infomercials and eat cereal in his underwear. No matter how many times he peed he still felt anxious. Around lunchtime, he and Seaver met up and rode down to the bridge where they were supposed to rendezvous with Jimmy. They found him leaning over the railing, staring at the water below, his shaggy black hair a curtain around his face. When they walked up to him, he didn't look away.

"You been here all night?" Seaver asked.

Still staring at the rust-colored water below, Jimmy asked: "Ever feel like it's you who's moving and not the water?"

DJ looked upriver, and Seaver must have as well, because he, too, fell silent for a time. Thunder rumbled overhead like the diarrheic growling of some giant gut. Distended and bruised, that gut was heavy with the impending flash flood that the radios were prognosticating when DJ had been in his kitchen, tying his shoes.

Jimmy showed them the ransom note just as DJ was starting to see what his friend had meant about the water. DJ recognized some of the letters Jimmy had cut out. The R in "Rice family," for instance, was from *The Lord of the Rings*. And one the Es was from a Goosebumps book. That gave DJ a chill. That Jimmy would use his own books instead of cutting up magazines and newspapers.

"What about you guys?" Jimmy said. They each showed Jimmy what he had instructed them to bring. Finally, Jimmy asked: "We ready to do this?"

They both nodded.

A Mack truck hauled past and the boys pumped their arms for the horn. The driver obliged their sacred request with a mighty honk-honk.

Jimmy hopped in the Radio Flyer hitched to DJ's mud-splattered Huffy and the three boys took off tearing up 226. Behind them the dark sky fissured with lightning. Jimmy turned on his boom box. The tape choked at first then blared: "For whom the bell tolls—time marches on! on! on!"

Thunder beat like hooves in their wake, but that portent went unheeded.

"Time marches on!"

Jimmy and Seaver both had to hold DJ back when he saw the Rice's trampoline. It seemed to him a portal to another world where flying was as common as walking. It called to him, a droning siren that had been buried beneath his subconscious and was now excavated to send him bounding across evolutionary gaps. Its canvas swallowed the sunshine like a black hole and mocked that implacable force gravity.

DJ eventually calmed down and the boys reported to their designated posts for surveillance.

Jimmy watched from underneath the Rice's porch. He had one of the two Darth Vader walkie-talkies DJ had been instructed to bring for the mission.

Seaver was up on Rice's garage roof with the other walkie-talkie.

DJ was swinging on the swing set across Choate Way, at the old school house, where the boys' dads had gone to elementary school.

On his reverse apex, DJ could see Chris Rice splashing around in his family's aboveground pool, getting in as much swimming as he could before the storm fell. Chris's mom was on the deck in her bathing suit, chewing gum into the cordless phone. Her skin made her look like a rotisserie chicken. Her bikini was like a faded dishcloth tied around the spot where boobs should be. Molly, Chris's mentally retarded older sister, walked her ten-speed around the yard, along her family's property line, as if there was some wall erected only she could see. She discussed matters of the neighborhood and agreed with herself in the same breath. As she went by the garage, DJ watched Seaver lean out and spit quietly into her bushy hair.

Lightning struck in the north and the precipitating thunderclap smacked the world into a potent silence.

Then came the barking of Priscilla, like the shrill clarion calls to signal the beginning of the end.

"Molly, let Priscilla out so she can pee before it storms," DJ heard Chris's mom say.

"Okay, mom," Molly said. She leaned her bike against the basketball hoop pole and ran through the yard to the Rice's brown-stained back porch. Once the dog was outside, Seaver stuffed into a piece of hotdog three of the little white pills that Salem took to sleep on bad nights. By DJ's next apex, Seaver was on one knee, taking aim with his slingshot. DJ jumped off as he swung forward. He landed on his bike and was out of the schoolyard in seconds. The grass could've been lava because never once did he touch it.

Seaver jumped down from the alley-side of the garage and met DJ on Choate Way.

"Did you see me spit in her hair?" Seaver asked.

DJ reached for the walkie-talkie.

Seaver stiff armed him away, and repeated his question into it at Jimmy.

"What'd you say, Chris?" they heard Chris's mom ask.

"What, mom?" Chris said. "What? Mom, what?"

"Shut up a second," Chris's mom said. "Thought I heard something."

"What was it?" Chris asked. "What did you hear, Mom?"

DJ looked at Seaver with hard intent.

"Mom. What do you think you heard?" Chris asked.

"Oh for Pete's sake, nothing!" Chris's mom said. "Get inside before it storms. Where's Priscilla? Priscilla!"

"Molly, find Priscilla and get inside. I got to run to the Countri-Mart for milk. I'll be home before Daddy. Make sure and close all the windows."

"Deej, put a tail on Mama Hen," Jimmy's voice said from the walkie-talkie. "Don't let her out of your sight. Take the walkie-talkie. Let us know when she's headed back. Remember: covert, stealth, espionage."

DJ snatched the walkie-talkie from Seaver. "Copy that."

"Seaver, once Mama Hen's gone, secure the chick. Roger?"

Seaver went to grab the walkie-talkie from DJ, but DJ twisted it away from him and said into it: "He says 'roger.' Out."

DJ waited until she was on Pecan St. before coming out from behind the garage to trail her. But then she made a left up 226. So she wasn't going to Countri-Mart, like she'd said. At least not right away.

She sped up the road, hell-bent to get somewhere, and if not for his eagle-vision, DJ might not have seen her make a right at the very top of town where Burnside faded into anonymous woodlands.

A fat raindrop landed on DJ's head, but he hardly noticed it. Chris's mom had entered the campground at the top of the hill. The camp was vacant until July. The white cabins stood scattered across the field like single-story, two-room mini-houses. Every one of their windows was intact and DJ couldn't believe he'd never thought to go up there before.

He rode on through the tiny ghost town, following the fresh tracks left by Chris's mom's Blazer. The tracks went toward the white tent-roofed church with a sign above its red doors that read "Silver Light Congregation." More raindrops bombed the dusty, drought-choked field, but the storm was still some way off, DJ hoped.

On the other side of the church, he saw Rice's blue Blazer idling.

Then he saw his dad's black F-150. The two of them, his dad and Chris's mom, were standing in-between their vehicles. He watched his dad grab Chris's mom by the arm and pull him into her. She made to resist, but DJ's dad wrapped her in both of his arms and pulled her in tighter.

DJ's bladder instantly swelled to rival the threatening sky above. It was so bad, he crossed his legs against pissing himself.

"Deej, you there?" the walkie-talkie in his back pocket suddenly squawked with Jimmy's voice. "Deej, abort! I repeat: abort mission! Don't follow Mama Hen. Get out—"

DJ grabbed at the walkie-talkie in his back pocket to turn it off, but he was too late. The adults had heard. His dad shouted: "Who's over there? Is that—?"

A bolt of lightning rent the sky and thunder cracked loud enough to shatter the world.

DJ was instantly on his bike, flying down the dirt road and out of the church camp. He quit the campgrounds and raced down the hill, getting low to minimize wind resistance. He reached for the walkie-talkie in his back pocket, to warn his friends, to see what had gone wrong with Operation Fearless, to just talk to someone he could trust. But when he realized the walkie-talkie wasn't there, that he'd dropped back at the church campgrounds, he wanted nothing more than to take off from his bike and fly far away.

But he had to warn his friends. In case they weren't already gone, it was up to him to get to the Rice's before the adults. He turned left onto Chestnut St., cut through yards, bunny-hopped lawn gnomes and shredded through flowerbeds to get back to Choate Way. He'd barely gotten to the mud alley when, out of dumb instinct, he bailed off his bike and ran toward the Rice's Lincoln Log-colored garage. He saw with some relief that the back parking lot was still empty, but knew he hadn't much time.

Seaver and Jimmy were nowhere to be seen. The Rice's backdoor was wide open.

DJ saw the trampoline. It called to him. He climbed onto to it, found its elastic surface nearly impossible to stand on. He tried to jump straight up into the air, but lost his balance and fell when the canvas gave in to his effort.

"Come on, man," DJ said to himself. "You got this. Obtain the bird's-eye vantage. Find your friends."

He started again, this time working his way up from tiny jumps. He found that keeping his legs straight helped. Soon, he was gaining height. Then he was higher than the Rice's garage and could see the swing set and the schoolyard. Then he was even higher than that where he saw on the horizon, the sun drowning in its own blood. He rocketed off the canvas to a great height and, in that moment, as he lingered at his zenith, DJ observed two things: first, that all around him were globules of rain, and inside them were tiny, inverted worlds ready to crash alongside him, and he saw on the deck of the pool, a garbage bag—the white kitchen bag he'd brought from home, per Jimmy's instructions.

He saw that the garbage bag was moving—at least whatever was inside it was moving and heading straight for the rain-dappled pool water.

DJ tucked his knees to absorb his bounce and launched off the trampoline. His legs were rubbery and walking on solid ground proved tricky.

Finally, the sky let loose. The rain fell like the ocean on Burnside that day.

DJ slipped on the wet lawn. Through the lattice, under the porch, he saw Seaver forcing Molly's hands down his pants.

DJ sprang to his feet. He reached the pool deck, smeared with mud, struggling to breathe through the curtain of rain.

The white trash bag floated on the surface of the water and at the bottom of the pool, curled into a shriveled ball was Priscilla. For a moment, before a thunder crash, DJ stared and wondered if it was the dog that was swaying beneath the water, or if it was himself.

The Blazer was still nowhere to be seen, so DJ quickly fished Priscilla out with the skimmer. He was on his knees to attempt mouth to mouth resuscitation when the fire hall's siren started wailing.

Seaver came out from under the porch like the siren was because of him. Molly came out after, her sweatpants down around her thighs. Seaver asked: "Where's Jimmy?"

"You should know," DJ shouted through the torrent.

"I was busy," Seaver said.

The rain fell like mortar. The bounty was gone. Seaver had compromised himself. The mission had failed. But DJ had finally flown on the trampoline, if only for a moment.

The best thing to do at that point was to hightail it out of there, he decided.

At the corner of Pecan and 226, right out in front of the Wethill's sagging mint-green house, a fire truck's oscillating red lights turned the rain into a shower of glowing blood. A crowd of Wethills had amassed around whatever was going on. They all stood looking at the ground. Silent, clutching themselves, dumb to the rain.

DJ elbowed his way through the crowd. Ryan Zenza, one of Burnside's volunteer firemen, a high school kid, tried to stop him. DJ stamped on his foot and circumvented that intercept.

There was the Blazer, idling cock-eyed in the middle of the road.

And there was Chris's mom, shaking like she was made of paper, eating her fingers.

An ambulance's siren bayed in the distance, but the other volunteer firemen only stood and looked down.

And on the rain-darkened road, some feet behind the Blazer, stripped of one of his braces and most of the skin on his face, there lay Jimmy. Blackened blood ran out from his right ear. The Darth Vader walkie-talkie was smashed into his hand, a crumple of white bones and black plastic. With one bulged-out eye that saw nothing and everything, he stared out past the crowd. Beyond the town, beyond the storm, into a different world. A world where flying was as common as walking.

DJ understood. Jimmy had gone there first, ahead of them, to light the way.

The Logic of Madness

Brian Serven

Shivering with excitement, Mr. Caldwell faces the gateway between Now and Forever.

He whispers, "Why should I be attached to anything . . . when nothing here is permanent?"

Mr. Caldwell stands, a silhouette before orange and pink clouds racing across a barren sky. The howling wind screams in agony, shaking leaves from trees, which cascade and fall in chaotic fits. The ocean rages with waves ripping and tearing at the rocks beneath the cliff where he stands. It's as if the sea herself were trying to pull Mr. Caldwell into her depths, to silence him.

Amidst this turmoil, he stands in defiance of all this illusion. He stands with a sense not of ending, but of renewal.

"If you want to have it all, you've got to let it all go," he recites in reassurance.

Pulling into their driveway, Mrs. Caldwell is surprised to see all the lights of their home on. Her husband's car is parked askew and the front door looks ajar. For all of his brilliance, he could be quite absentminded with the little things.

She parks, collects the groceries, and walks by his car, smiling as once again she's found his keys in the ignition. Nearing the door, she hears the last song on his favorite record playing, recognizing that this means he is likely lost among his books and journals, scribing indiscernible reflections that would eventually be thread together into an incomprehensible masterpiece.

She quietly enters and slips passed his office door, which is open a crack, making her way into the kitchen where the groceries find their home. She prefers not to bother him when he is working and proceeds to prepare dinner.

The last song ends. Silence ensues. The typical sounds could not be heard, his pacing, his exclamations, the shuffling to put another record on. Instead there is deafening silence.

"William," she calls out.

Silence.

"William?"

She lays the knife upon the cutting board, wipes her hands on her apron, and walks toward the office.

"Will? Hello?"

Pausing, listening, still hearing nothing, she nudges the door open.

Suddenly, her home, her safe place, her security and sense of stability escape her as the door eerily creaks open. Her stomach turns, her voice quivers as she calls out "Will!"

Gazing into his office leaves her feeling alarmed. Instead of its usual state of organized chaos, the room is orderly. Walking in she notices the books aren't laying open or in towering stacks, the papers aren't strewn across the floor in acts of inspiration, the records aren't piled next to the record player, everything is in its proper place. The room looks like a museum. His executive desk in all its authority is empty, except for a small scrap of paper, a note from her husband that reads:

Sometimes everything is so perfectly aligned
there's no longer a need to decide, no choices left
It's all so effortless
There is no divide between 'One' and everything else
no separation of mind and body
Wholeness is attainable
This is one of those moments
It's the clarity you hear about
that peering through the mist, the Awakening
And I've got to tell you
it truly is bliss
The final and absolute resolution
that complete surrender
This is the liberation I've read about

These cliffs are home to Mr. Caldwell. They inspire such timeless reflection. There is hardly enough space to think in that confining and static office. Here is sheer boundlessness. The great expanse of sea and heaven invites the most profound and prolific daydreaming. No place has ever felt more enlightening.

Mr. Caldwell instructs himself quietly, "Before liberation, one must face his demons, see through his own darkness . . . slay his past."

Stumbling toward the edge of the cliff, crouching, peering at the jagged rocks below, he turns his back toward the great chasm. Struggling to stand upright, gazing upward he nearly loses his equilibrium, sending a great surge of anxiety through his abdomen. Finding his balance, closing his eyes he begins to recall his youth. The winds try ceaselessly to force him off the cliff, thunder roars shaking the earth, and waves reach and reach but fail to drag him in.

Fragmented memories flash in symbols and snapshots in his mind. *The past never escapes us,* he thinks. *No matter how much we try to hide it away, to burn it down to ashes, to accept it, its potency, its grip on our throats never lessens, we're never free.* He drops to his knees. *Take me, take me, choke this life from me, take me . . . please.*

That debilitating darkness, inadequacy, hopelessness and helplessness, residing deep in his being induces the deepest sorrow, the deepest fear and deepest despair. Those indefinable moments, shards of experience that shape the very essence of a perceived soul, bind it in the blackest pits of agony. Mr. Caldwell, despite his suffering, doesn't falter, doesn't let this darkness shake him.

The belief grows that suffering could be conquered if one had the courage to face and welcome Death. Overcoming the fear, the burden of *knowing* but not acting. This was all coming to an end here, now. The courage is here. The time is now. A bolt of lightning strikes the rocks beneath the cliff. Digging down into a strength he never knew he had, he rises to his feet, clenches his fists, and crushes these feelings, forcing them into an internal abyss.

Mr. Caldwell is left standing boldly as the nature around him grows quiet along with the nature within. Turning toward the void, he sits, head bent forward in immense relief.

With her hand covering her mouth, her eyes welling with tears, poor Mrs. Caldwell freezes with terror. A voice inside her head says, *move!* causing her to dart out of the office, through the kitchen, and onto the patio. Looking toward the sea, she knows where he went. She pulls out her cell phone, speed-dials, and in a moment the line opens.

"Hello Susan."

"It's Will. He's at the cliffs . . . . "

"Did he stop his medication?"

"Damn it, John! Get over here!"

"On my way. Try to stay calm. Your worry will only exacerbate his condition."

"Hurry!"

Mr. Caldwell feels light, vibrant, and youthful. He feels more joy than he has ever felt before. Without thinking he spontaneously begins to dance and hum. He indulges for a moment in his unbridled jubilation. He imagines his lovely wife in his arms and remembers his next hindrance.

He thinks about how running and hiding from fears and all the darkness in the world is no way to live; that's not freedom. Though neither is clinging to all the pleasures and joys. These things too keep you from true liberation; they create their own fear—fear of loss.

He whispers, "If you want to have it all, you've got to let it all go."

Mr. Caldwell thinks about his wife, the smell of the back of her neck as he remembers nestling up next to her each night. Remembering those undefined moments and flashes of her laugh and all its spontaneity. Her unforgettable smile which was the first feature of immense attraction. The look in her eyes when she tries so hard to understand and her brilliantly simple questions that provide so much clarity. The tears of joy at their wedding and all the lovely life-inspiring hope. As he recalls these memories, these impressions, he endeavors to observe how they affect him. *This love isn't bad,* he thinks. *It's just fleeting. It passes and with the end of time, it will all pass.*

Mr. Caldwell thinks about eternity, about moments of clarity in beams of sunlight illuminating his consciousness, the same light shining through leaf-filled trees with mesmerizing color. He thinks about myths and legends, shadows and mysteries, and all the things that caused him to pause and wonder.

"Let go," he whispers. "Just let it all go."

Considering, in what feels like a great silence amidst a raging storm, that true liberation comes from want and need of nothing. Freedom is purest without these attachments. Wholeness can't be found in illusions. When it's all recognized as flickers of light and specks of dust. Then one can become everything all at once. One can become absolute.

The cell phone drops to the stone patio with pieces exploding in all directions. In a panic Mrs. Caldwell sprints from the patio, through her beloved flowerbeds, crushing orchids and dahlias, across the yard and toward the edge of the forest. Ducking a branch at the entrance of the narrow path, she slips on pine needles and falls, crashing into dead and broken lower branches. The fear overrides the pain. She bolts down the path toward the cliff. Gnarled, protruding roots and jagged rocks fail to slow her down. She'd never dream to walk this path at night, in this darkness, but love and rationality don't mix. She sees the skyline at the end of the path just ahead. Her mind races, she doesn't know what she'll do if he isn't there. She thinks of closing her eyes and just running until the earth beneath her feet cracks and crumbles. That is, if her heart doesn't explode in her chest before she makes it through the woods.

Mr. Caldwell stands in defiance of all his suffering, above and beyond all of his trivial joys. He stands a man who has given up his place in this world. A man who has nothing left to say, feel, or ponder. It is all coming together for him now, that Great Everything beckoning him, that Great Nothing beckoning him. He stands within reach of bridging the gap between the transitory and the real. From the impermanent and the permanent. From the illusion and the pure.

He feels his tired muscles and weak bones, his heart struggling to pump blood, his lungs fighting to draw in his weary breath. He feels each nervous synapse and singular cell function. He bids farewell to this worn vessel. His senses, dull and misguiding, begin to falter. It feels as if his whole body is breaking apart at a subatomic level. The cliff seems to have disappeared, he feels weightless, as if enveloped by absolute darkness. His mind goes blank, a total flatline, there is nothing left to consider.

Yet before total black out, before complete absorption, a brief fluctuation of mind reacts to a sound that breaks this divine silence. It's the call of his name, his wife's voice. All this disintegration jolts back into a full body experience. His eyes open, he feels the fall. He's completely aware as he collides with forever.

All this darkness breaks as Mrs. Caldwell stumbles from the

woods. The clouds have passed, the seas have simmered, and the wind has eased. She kneels, knowing without looking that her dear William is gone, he's crossed over.

Instead of looking down at the jagged rocks and sea, she looks up toward the stars. She hears his voice in memory, that quote "If you want to have it all, you've got to let it all go." Her agony transitions toward acceptance.

She rises and stands defiantly, turning her back on the great void. She recalls her suffering, her clinging, and her whole life experience. Soon, she too feels vibrant and light, she feels whole . . . .

"I am ready, darling. Here I come."

Dr. Petrie pulls up to the house, sighs, and gets out of his car. He follows the walkway to the backyard of the Caldwell home. He walks, shining his flashlight all around the path through the woods. He glances at his watch bothered by the hour, considering how these "episodes" never cease to interrupt his sleep.

"Will?" he calls out. "Susan?"

Eventually Dr. Petrie comes to the clearing, stepping out onto the cliff. He looks down toward the rocks and sea and sees nothing. Seemingly unmoved he sits collecting his breath and thoughts. He reaches into his breast pocket and pulls out a small book. Opening the cover he finds his own words: *Will, the past is dead, the future is speculation, all you have is now. Let go my friend. If you want to have it all, you've got to let it all go.*

Closing the book, he remembers the last meeting with Mr. Caldwell, how relieved he seemed, how liberated. How, when he left, he'd dropped this little book, this gift, into the trash, then turned, smiled, and left.

Head low, Dr. Petrie stands. Turning to walk back into the woods, he nonchalantly flings the book into that gateway between Now and Forever.

66 *The Healing Monsters*

Lamey Neljor

Jessica Pimentel

Sitting
Shrouded in black
Now is the time Not
time to smile Not
time to cry
but time . . . .

I take the seven steps.

Sitting silently
the world becomes so loud.
Each drip. Each drop. Each breath bends the air.
Come to this place. Come to me. I ***invoke*** you with all my being.
In my blood there is a burning.

I am blinded by the magnificence that suddenly faces me. A light inconceivable in purity and power.

Countless aeons you were here. Countless aeons I beg you to

remain. I ***beseech***
you; stay before me. "Please stay with me," I plead.
Stay close to me. Over me. Around me. Inside me.
In my body there is a sickness.

I fall to my knees at your feet. My face happily, humbly in the dirt.
The only way I am worthy enough to be here. I ***prostrate*** to your majesty. Your words hang off
my ears like jewels. Your face brushes lightly across my mind changing the very course of the ocean in which I drown.
Gaze at me with loving eyes. Whisper in my ear your wisdom. Hold the diamond before me.
Cut me with your sword. I give myself to you. I am yours. Crush me.
In my heart there is a darkness.

An ***offering*** set forth before you of things both familiar and impossible.
My gifts in the ether, set in the vastness of clouds magnified by the mind's eye. Cultivated in the
garden of my dreams. I strip myself of all possession and pretense. Everything I have is yours
including my life. My friends. My enemies. The strangers. The things that bring me joy and
pain. My vices and desires. Bracelets and shackles ripped off my wrist. Without hesitation I
give them to you. My sacrifice. Take it all. Take it all away
In my flesh there is a weakness.

I cannot bear this anymore. If I were to ***confess*** each deed there would be no time left to
count the times. This iniquity running through me. Holding me. It takes my lips, my
tongue, my fingertips, my hands, my body. The arch in my back. The glance in my eye. It
takes my thoughts till I have no control. Delighting in suffering it grows and grows. It does its will through me.
Take them all from me as a collection. You know each secret and every detail. I can tell
them to you one by one. But you were there. You know me well. My time left here is short and uncertain.
In my mind there is a poison.

No longer concerned with gain or loss—with praise, blame, fame, or obscurity. Suffering and
pleasure are one and the same to you. This was not an easy task. All this you have done for
me. I ***rejoice*** at your mastery of the eight.
You've shown me the way. I see what lies ahead . . . liberation and the fight. No other
choice. There is no doubt. White light in. Black smoke out.
In the air there is a wish.

May the struggles I endure . . . may the foes that cross my path . . . .
May this nightmare dream awake. All that I have gathered I ***dedicate*** . . . .
May they be of service—myself, my acts, my thoughts. Each victory and defeat single

pointedly towards this one goal. Each moment of illusion to break free.

In the heavens there is void

Precious one! Come over me. Come into me. Be one with me. I
request
you bestow upon me the ultimate result.
Your gifts of the three places. Upon three doors I knock. Three times three times three times three places . . . .
In the earth there is a fear.

Lightning white envelops me. A stream of light pours into me and splits my skull right
through the moon that rests atop there silently, right through me with such force the ground
below me cracks open . . . .

In that crack I see the Lord of Death. A smile upon his face. His lascivious breath bated and
hungry . . . waiting for me to fall . . . licking the beads of sweat that trickle into the crevice of
his lips and teeth. Four gnashing fangs to greet me.

This is what he wants. Feed him.
Heaven and earth. Blood and flesh. Body, mind, and heart.

The light rains down. Reigns down. Pours through. Nectar.
Destroying an army of demons inside and around me . . . leaving not one . . . and the
Lord of Death stands there smiling. Waiting. Wanting. More.

The nectar washes over me. Through me.
Blue, white, yellow, red, green.
Through every hole, every opening, every pore is purged. I am vile.
Snakes, scorpions, worms, and spiders escaping, crawling out from my mouth, nose and ears falling into his laughing throat.
He thrashes. He rages. He wants. More.
Every hole, every opening, every pore is scoured. I am disgusting. My filth
drips out of me. I cover him in my putridity.
In blood and bile. In puss and phlegm. Five forms of waste delighting him. Tar . . . slow . . . to mud . . . mud. . . to smoke . . . smoke to light . . . .
His mouth . . . agape, tilted upwards, catching each drop. Licking his face. Loving each taste.
Satisfied.
The ground beneath me closes.
Sealed with diamonds.

Examining myself I am stainless.
Each nerve from root to tip, each sinew, each drop, each breath is crystalline radiance.
Yet in my heart darkness remains. Just one last bit. A subtle trace. Master
takes up his sword to touch that spot
plunging deeply.
Finishing the rest.
He dissolves into me.
The darkness is no more.
No pain.

No sadness.
No sickness. No fear.
No feeling. No form.
I am no more.

Gone.

Isn't Much to Tell

Dustin LaValley

Ah, Jesus, you again. I thought they'd send someone new this time but whatever. Huh? I don't know, there isn't much else to tell. Really? I don't see why I should share that with you but, well, all right. I'll try . . . . It'll kill some time anyway so why not.

I grew up in a foster home. I wasn't in foster care, my parents ran a home. I have two older sisters, both about a decade older than me. Me, I'm the baby of the family. At any time, from birth to twelve, thirteen years old I was surrounded by foster brothers and two adopted brothers. All older, teenagers when I was just a kid. They were straight out of juvenile centers, places for teens too young for prison who had committed crimes hard enough to make the worst criminals cringe. Thieves and brawlers, bad eggs from childhood whose parents just gave up, violence seemed to be inborn to these guys.

But my parents, they set 'em straight from the first day. My father is a small man, but wide, muscular. He'd work 6-2 at the max facility upstate, fighting the real gangbangers, the dudes doing life with nothing to lose, working out and starting fights at a cockeyed glance and waiting their turn to fuck up a CO at their best convenience.

He'd come home from the prison and workout, lift weights and go for a jog, bring the boys with him, me included. They'd do six-to-eight miles a day, I'd do about two before one of the boys was put in charge of escorting me home while the others continued.

You learn and discover a lot growing up in such place. Heavy metal . . . Guns N' Roses, Pantera, Sepultura, Metallica . . . these guys, I was listening to as a child, learning the lyrics and learning the meaning of the lyrics. Thrash, hardcore, punk . . . anything heavy and fast, seems I discovered it before those oh-so-sensitive teenage angst years. Nirvana, teen angst? No, no, no. Minor Threat, Black Flag, D.R.I., Agnostic Front; these guys showed angst, not that whiny-sissy shit that came in the '90s. Fuck, even Beastie Boys. They were rocking the New York hardcore circuit back in the '80s. You know that? Didn't think so. What? Yeah, of course the music had an impact on me, that's why I'm talkin' about them. Shit . . . and no, I don't think so, so don't get me started on that fucking music leading to violence bullshit. Ain't true.

I learned about loyalty, I learned about blood, about trusting no one but yourself and relying on no one but yourself. I was taught to hate, to be self-reliant and most importantly, how to fight. I never had a fight with one of the boys but we'd rough house. I had gloves on my hands soon as I could stand on my own two feet. When you've played football with guys thrice your size and had your nose broken so many times that your mother, a nurse, taught you how to adjust it yourself, you're pretty much set when shit went down on the playground. I'm a small guy,

140 pounds, 5'7" as I speak, was always a small kid. The bullies, the fat, dumb kids, when they'd spot you and corner you, the last thing they were expecting was to be leaving that situation unconscious, left eye swollen shut and missing a few teeth . . . if they were lucky enough that I hadn't broken their jaw. My right hand, it's always been heavy.

When you're working out and training toe-to-toe with guys twice your age and thrice your size, a little shitass punk fourth grader is as much a worry as an alien invasion. Ducking hook, that was my weapon of choice and never once did it fail me. I never started a fight in my life but I've finished every one of them. When I got sent home from school, they knew I didn't start it, therefore there was no punishment. You can't punish your son for protecting himself. Reminds me of when I was a Cub Scout, that little organization before becoming a Boy Scout. I was in there for about a month, doing a bunch of girly shit. I wanted to play with fire, go camping and get that fucking knife. I never did. We had father-son cake bakes and puppet shows . . . Jesus fuck, the puppet show.

There was only one in that month and I refused to participate, and when the scoutmaster's son got mouthy with me for not being part of it, not being a team player, he got a fist in the mouth. I was kicked out. I'm positive my father left that night, that basement, the proudest father of them all. Leaving behind all the poor fuckers watching their boys play with hand-puppets, secretly wishing they'd spent more time teaching their kid how to hold his guard instead of plopping them down in front of the idiot box with a family-size bag of Twizzlers and a bottle of Pepsi.

There were tough kids, like me, tough but no brawlers.

Recess had ended one day in about fourth grade, we formed a line, all the kids. I got in my place and received a knock in the back of the head, I spun around and caught the kid behind me with a hook to the cheekbone. Jason Lavine, a new kid, never seen him before that day, before that punch. He just looked at me, his head didn't turn, his expression was blank, kinda one of those *what the fuck?* looks, ya know? I stared at him for a second wondering if he was going to reply, then suddenly his right hand caught me in the face, my reaction was a mimic of his. Turns out, this little runt bastard Josh Nichols clocked me in the back of the head, then hid behind the taller boy. I let it slide. Jason and I from that day became friends, not good friends, but we hung out from time to time. Josh, that little fucker, I got a story about him.

He was a jokester, thought he was at least, always trying to cause some trouble for a chuckle. Little fucker he was, I was small but this kid was a fucking runt. If he was a piglet he'd have been killed off. He sat behind me and one day he had big-kid scissors and wanted to show them off. Silently he leaned forward and clipped my shirt collar, right next to my neck. I said something to him, a warning. A moment later, I felt the scissors back against my shirt and I stood, spinning around, grabbing his outstretched arm with my left hand and grasping the back of his head with my right. I pulled his arm forward and at the same time, smashed his face off the edge of the desk. Ya know the ones, the ones where the chair and desk are welded together. His face hit that corner and he fell back in his seat when I let him go. Apparently the teacher had seen this all play out, I sat back down at my desk while Josh, barely with it, was sent to the nurse then to the principle. His scissors were confiscated.

While I'm on it, I'll say a little about Nate. Nate Bowman was a badass, plain and simple. We used to do the Gauntlet in gym to test our abilities— climbing rope to the ceiling, Nate and I did it without using our feet, the only two kids in the school who could even reach the top and we used only our arms. There were tires to run through, push-ups and pull-ups and a one-mile run plus some random crap to navigate, monkey bars and that sort of thing. Well, Nate was always ahead of me, just by a fraction. I'd do sixty-four push-ups in a minute, Nate would do sixty-five. I'd do fifteen pull-ups before dismounting the bar, Nate would do sixteen. He was almost my size, a little bigger, quiet and picked on a lot for being poor. Not by me, no, I was just as poor wearing a hand-me-down Bad Brains t-shirt and I never considered myself poor. One day my best buddy of my childhood years got into a fight on the playground and me being me, I made sure the other kid was put to the ground before my buddy could get hurt, but before I could regain myself after tossing the kid to the sand, I was on the ground myself. Nate had my arm locked up and my face in the sand. He yelled. Told me to never touch his brother and he'd never touch me. He didn't have to let me up, he could have beat the shit outta me right there but he didn't. We became friends. We, along with Jason, became the kids whose names were known throughout the city school system by kids in other schools, names not to fuck with once middle school came.

Nate moved when high school started, I didn't hear from him or about him until the war in the Middle East. He had joined the army, his unarmored Humvee hit an IED and Nate didn't make it. A shame, he was a good kid, a good guy.

When I was a bit older, the start of my teen years the boys began moving out and I found myself alone. All that was left was the skills, the music, and knowledge they had shared with me. At that age I began riding BMX, Bicycle Moto-Cross, twenty-inchers, ya know, those little bikes kids do tricks on. I got pretty fucking good, I was sponsored and did some competitions and won a few times, but that's overkill.

There was a crew of us, about ten or so that rode every day until the snow came. We got chased by the pigs on every one of those goddamn days and if not the pigs, the toy-pigs, the security guards. We enjoyed it. They never caught us, we were too fast, too skilled. If a piggy was on your ass, best bet was to pop a 180 and haul ass in the other direction, ninety-nine percent of the time piggy fell on his curly-tailed ass in some awkward skid-turn shit he thought was flashy on his big-boy bike. Cruisers on us, even better. Hop a curb, cross through a few yards, toss the bike over a fence . . . . We knew the streets like the back of our hands and we loved the chase, the thrill, and most of the time we actually beckoned it.

During the day we usually rode dirt, hit up the trails with a boom box on battery power and something heavy and fast to get us pumped . . . most of us preferred Pennywise. That shit got you moving! On the trails, smooth sailing in a train, up and down, bobbing and weaving, nothing big, just flow and style. When night came, we rode the city streets. That's where the trouble came from. Drunken college kids, rich suburban sissy-boys in their parents' Volvos tossing beer cans at us, not expecting to find us dropping our bikes and ready to throw our fists around.

One I remember most is this time we were riding downtown, about four of us and this Ford Bronco pulls up and suddenly some huge meathead and his black twin jump out, before we knew what was up they were throwing punches. Adam, he was a tough kid, he took meathead down, slapping away his punches and landing solid hooks. The black dude, well me and Dan see him coming at us and we ghost our bikes into the Bronco and charge him. With us both using all our weight we got him up against the Bronco's passenger side and held him there, landed a few punches to his gut. To this day I have no clue why they stopped but they sure as shit didn't expect a few punk kids to whoop 'em. But before we could do much damage some random woman pulled up and began screaming, thinking us, the weird looking guys taking names, were the provokers. We ignored her until she got out and tried to physically stop us, then we backed away and got on our rides and left. Last thing we wanted was to accidently hit a woman. Though she was in the wrong, that's still no reason.

I was raised to respect women, even if they by all means deserve it, never lay a hand on a woman. Every day on that Hoffman Sugarbaby with my crew was a fight, a fight to get away from the pigs, a fight with random passersby who thought we were easy targets. So many fights, so many brawls, so many good memories . . . man, how I could go on and on here . . . .

High School was when I really began to take a change. I was the quiet kid in the corner with the Snapcase t-shirt and frayed jeans, skater shoes and the *you don't fuck with me, I don't fuck with you attitude.* A lot of guys challenged that.

All of them wished they hadn't . . . .

I spoke when spoken too, I did my work and I kept to myself. I can't remember a time when I talked shit ever and when I was done with a situation, never was a word muttered. I broke teeth, jaws, eye-sockets. I used books and backpacks as impromptu weapons for self-defense. Every week, a new jock or pretty boy acted up, messed with me, day after day until he felt I was broken down enough to finish by hand and that's when the redundancy should have shown all the rest not to fuck with the little guy with no friends, all the zits, and the Acid Bath hoodie. But they kept coming and one after the other they fell.

Take this asshole Thomas Rich, he's a white kid now in his thirties still trying to make it as a gangsta rapper, we have a name for them, we call them Paper Gangsters. Well anyways, one day Thomas decides he doesn't like me and starts calling me names, "faggot," "pussy," "homo," ya know, all the shit that those types of secret homosexuals use to try and hurt you. The days pass, he ups the level to shoulder nudges in the hallway, I let it slide with a smile, waiting for it. Just waiting for it and waiting with a smile, hoping he makes the next move.

And he does.

One day as school is let out I'm leaving the main entrance and he calls me out amongst a good sized crowd of peckerheads and sluts, they all find his bashing a bit funny and when I don't acknowledge him, he puts a hand on me, tries turning me around, cheered on by the others. That hand on me . . . that was his last chance.

I spun around and with my backpack dangling on one shoulder, let it swing with my momentum and socked that fucker right in the face, an upward swing. He stumbled backwards, dazed, I dropped the bag and pounced. He was tall, I was short, he was big framed and I was small framed, and I bent right over and got under his center with my shoulder under his naval and my arms wrapped around his legs, pulling forward with my hands in the pits of his knees I took him down in the middle of the crowd. I crawled up like a spider monkey and put a knee in his sternum and held his arm down with my left and began landing bone-crunching rights all over his face. The more he twisted and turned the more targets I was given. By the time I was pulled off by some male faculty his nose was broken, he lost a few teeth and both eyes were black, purple, and shut. And as for me, my knuckles were cut up pretty badly from his pearly whites but the adrenaline kicking through me lasted long after the pigs left me in my parents care.

Damn.

I bet I was the only kid in that school to make a shiv in the bathroom stall, using a lighter and some duct tape and paintbrushes I stole from art class. I guess I'll mention that one quick. A few of the roided up gymrats on the football team had promised me a good beating one day after sticking up for one of the Type O Negative, KMFDM type goth kids they were fucking with, so I took to making a homemade knife a few classes before school was let out.

At the end of the day I hadn't seen any of them cunts. Most likely they were too busy taking turns on some blonde, bubblegum popping, hair-twirling cheerleader down behind the staircase as the coach secretly watched. Sirlo was his name, fucking wall-eyed prick, wish I had gotten a chance to get him too.

Oh well . . . .

So now you can see a pattern here can't you? I wasn't out looking to hassle anyone. I stayed to myself, didn't bother nobody, liked my bike and heavy music and if trouble found me and it gave me a shove, I shoved back, sometimes more than necessary but never was I first to drum up a situation.

By now I'm assuming you can sense my misanthropic

cynicism had grown bigger than that lazy sack of shit who Jerry Springer had to knock the bedroom wall down with a bulldozer to get him out of the house. Damn, remember that!? Crazy! Reminds me of that episode of *The Simpsons* where Bart imagines himself as a lardo who washes himself with a rag on a stick . . . ha! Ah man, I'm ranting . . . . I'll get back on it so you can keep scribbling in that prissy notepad of yours with that prissy pen I bet cost more than a pair of Levi jeans.

A lot of guys here, they'd all cry about their childhoods, their families, being touched by their uncles or taking candy from strangers with moustaches, some crap excuse for their time instead of manning up. Not me. I had a good childhood, I loved it, wish I could go back and live it again. No one touched me, I knew what molestation was. I had good family that would never do that sort of thing anyway and I wasn't some dummy kid hopped up on sugar. And I'm not going to use that lame, "It's society's fault!" bullshit I always hear.

Fuck that. I liked it. All that hurt. All those years dealing out pain, blood, and broken bone that could have been avoided if they had only left me be, all that began to build up in me, it turned me, like a vampire turns a human, it turned me. I began to like to hurt and as ya know . . . I know ya know I know ya know, that what I did to get here, that was all 'cause I liked doing it.

It's like that hostage thing, what's it called? When they start to— yeah, that's it, Stockholm Syndrome. It was like that, I guess, for lack of better words. The more it was dealt to me, the more I accepted it and then it became me and when it became me, the more I wanted and the more I got the more I did and then, needless to say, I stopped caring and went for it stupidly . . .

. . . we know I'm not stupid, I know you have papers in that folder with my IQ tests, my MENSA membership, my state tests, those DAT tests they give to kids. A man with a 163 IQ thinks things through, I'm no borderline 'tard like the rest of these window-lickers, when I finish my push-ups, my dips, pull-ups, Burpees, ya know my routine . . . I sit back in my bunk and read. Doesn't matter what or who, anything, anyone. Barry Gifford, Washington Irving, Hemmingway, Jerry Stahl, Palahnuik, Steve Erickson, Eric Miles Williamson, whoever.

I fucked up. Maybe I wanted to fuck up, maybe you think that. But I doubt it. Plain and simple, I fucked up. I grabbed that spic gangbanger in broad daylight, saw him slap his bitch up good and as I know ya know, you don't hit women and like all my skeletons, they had it coming. Isn't one of them fourteen motherfuckers who didn't deserve it. Gangbanger punks, lazy ass drive-by sissies killing innocent kids, drug dealing scumbags, lady pimping sissy men with heavy hands, child molesters, free-lance gynecologists . . . .

They all had their reasons to be dealt such torturous and long, drawn-out deaths and I was doing good. Better than any of them pigs out there; city, county, state, federal, better than any of them but I knew all along that I slip once and I'm fucked and that's exactly what happened.

I saw that spic hit her and my blood boiled, I sped through that red light and squealed to a stop, socked him in the head with a retractable baton and tossed him limp and bleeding from his temple wound in the back seat, so overwhelmed with hate and rage, red in my eyes so strong all those witnesses were invisible to me and lucky for that cocksucker the pigs ran me down before I could get home and tie him up in the cellar for a wire hanger whipping and finger snipping for him to bleed out slow.

They say hate breeds rage. Don't they? Whatever, I think some band, yeah, Cutthroat said that . . . .

Anyway, they say hate breeds rage but I guess with my story—I see by your fidgetiness and how you keep eyeing that overpriced piece of tin on your wrist that we're about done—they can say . . . well, I guess they can say whatever they want 'cause I don't have anything witty here to add.

Now, if you're done scribbling down the dictation summery of my short-winded life story I'm sure the COs would love to get me back in my box, do their head count and head home to their families and next time, maybe next time if you're good and bring me that fucking vanilla Charleston Chew bar, Decibel Magazine, iPod Shuffle loaded with Helmet and Unsane like I asked of you, asked of you ever so politely, I'll begin to tell you where the bodies are.

October Wedding

Jesse Bullington

The light snow abated as the carriage left the gate of the manse, and what leaves remained in the wood shone as the dying sun emerged from the clouds. The Baron looked at Erzsébet's veiled face and wondered where she had instructed the driver to take them. The next day they would be married, and her request for a ride in the forest on the eve before wasn't in itself unusual—it was the date that bothered him.

Ten years to the day since he was first wed, ten years precisely. Initially curious at the notion of courting again, he was then elated by the prospect; now, with the sun slipping into the boughs overhead, he felt the trembling of some other, lesser known emotion. He looked again at his intended, and she might have smiled under her veil.

She looked almost exactly like her sister. While Angéla was alive he had of course met Erzsébet countless times, and on these occasions he had always marveled at the similarity. Though Angéla was a year her senior, the girls were as identical as two blossoms on a vine, each pale and flawless, with the faint perfume of clove and rose.

Their father had scowled at him from the doorway, the same scowl he always bestowed upon the Baron. He had disliked the Baron even before his marriage to Angéla, and her death, no matter the circumstances, had changed the rivalry to a simmering hatred. And yet the withered old fool had granted him Erzsébet's hand, a fact as perplexing as it was invigorating.

Five lonely years the Baron had spent in his keep, five years of wandering cold hallways and empty rooms. How he had missed Angéla, her quiet voice, her delicate touch, her earnest moans and squeals. Even her cruelty he missed, that malicious sense of humor that irked him to no end was now one of his dearest memories. He dreamed of her often, always waking as she screamed, her wails fading into the howling of wolves outside the gate.

He would stand alone in their special room for hours, lost in his memories. But no more, he thought. Soon the room's black candles would be exchanged for a roaring fire, the cold bed alive and warm once more. With Erzsébet.

Peering out the window, the Baron saw they approached his keep. He hid his smile by stroking his chin. He had told her they would travel wherever she wished, through field and forest, village and hills, and she had chosen his home. As the tiered roofs came into view, he reflected how on the following night they would make the same approach as man and wife.

Erzsébet was quieter than her sister, though he had yet to discern if she were introspective or simply shy. It excited him, this coyness. She sat up and leaned to the open window, her veil brushing his cheek. He turned to face her, but she leaned passed him and called out to the driver.

"Stop at the gate." She settled back in her seat, her teeth

flashing under the lace webbing.

"I thought we might," the Baron shifted, sweat beading his brow. "That is, aren't we going in?"

The coach slowed to a stop.

"Won't you open the door for me?" Her voice was sweet as the port he favored after an evening's sport.

He obliged, unsure of what she had in mind. A walk around the walls of the keep? Surely not, it was overgrown and rocky, no place for a soft girl in softer clothes.

She talked with the driver as the Baron clambered out of the cabin. Over the years of solitude his muscled form had thickened with fat, and he was vaguely annoyed to leave his seat.

"Is that all right then, sir?" The coachman raised his wooly eyebrows at the Baron.

"What?" The Baron asked.

"I told him to go inside to his wife, so we might ride alone." Erzsébet smiled.

"But how will we ride without a driver? Surely Paul can mind his ears, so it will be as if we are alone?"

Erzsébet shook her head. "I'll drive. I can handle the carriage as well as Paul, and there's room enough for us both on the coachboard."

The Baron looked uncertainly at her.

"Please, husband?" she whispered as she took his hand in hers, and his resistance fled.

"Go home, Paul," the Baron said, his heart beating faster.

The coachman shrugged and hopped from the carriage. Erzsébet leaned back as she pulled her veil off, tossing it inside the coach and shutting the door. She turned back to the Baron.

"Won't you help me up?"

As she climbed atop the carriage he steadied her legs, her thighs warm beneath her embroidered dress. He laboriously scaled the side after her, settling onto the coachboard. A breeze stirred the dead leaves around the carriage, lifting Erzsébet's dark hair around her face so it tickled his ear.

Erzsébet turned the carriage around and drove it back down the hill into the wood. The Baron bounced uncomfortably on the hard seat but was too eager to please his bride to complain. He had never ridden atop his coach before, and it was a bit exhilarating despite the discomfort, the cool air-drying his sweat.

She leaned forward, urging the horses faster. The leaves whipped around them as they broke from the main road onto a smaller track. The Baron dug his hands into the coachboard, worried they might be thrown from the vehicle.

The sun gave no warmth as it descended through the branches, the wind picking up and cutting through the Baron's fur-lined cloak. The path split again, and again she took the narrower avenue. Here the wood thickened, closing in around the coach like a great arboreal hall. The boughs hung so low that several times the Baron had to duck to avoid losing his hat.

The path curved, but Erzsébet urged the horses on at the same pace, and for a moment the carriage went up on two wheels as it rounded the bend. This was too much for the Baron, who had grown nauseated.

"Stop," he said quietly, and when she didn't respond, he almost shouted, "stop!"

She didn't stop, but slowed the horses to a walk so quickly the Baron slid forward and almost fell. The horses ambled though the trees, which had thinned a bit. He turned to Erzsébet, his heart slowing.

"Do you always drive them so?" he asked.

"Usually much faster." She winked at him, her green eyes like mossy pools.

Turning forward, he realized they had left the path and cut across a clearing in the forest.

"Where are we going?" he demanded, his patience at its limit.

"The belly of the wood." She smiled enigmatically, again reminding him so much of Angéla he had to shake his head to banish the specter of his dead wife. He was about to ask her what she meant when she asked a question of her own.

"Why do you think I wish to marry you?"

It caught him off guard, and he looked at her in bafflement.

"I don't know," he answered honestly. "Love, perhaps?"

She laughed, the horses leading them out of the meadow and back into the trees.

"Then for the sake of your parents," he said, annoyed at her mocking tone.

"My parents hate you," she said, ever smiling.

His stomach turned. What game was she at? Angéla had been fond of such mean-spirited riddles, and it worried him that her sister shared this defect.

"Why do you think I've taken us all the way out here, at dusk, so far away from any sort of help?" She asked, bringing the horses to a halt. The wood had grown thick around them, the sun level with the coachboard through the screen of underbrush.

"I don't know," he looked sternly at her.

"Perhaps I've a secret lover who conspired with me to murder you in the forest, and he now waits in yonder thicket." She motioned to the tangle of small yews in front of them, their naked branches twisted round each other.

The Baron swallowed, his heart accelerating again.

"Or perhaps my father and his men, to avenge my sister?" The air was still and cold, her breath clouding the air, mixing with his. At the mention of Angéla the chill left him, his skin seeming to ignite. He had known they must talk of her, but never imagined they would do so in such a strange place. He anxiously looked around in the twilight, but nothing stirred among the rotting leaves and patches of earth-stained snow.

"I—I," the Baron stammered, for the first time in his life at a loss for words.

Erzsébet laughed, stroking his cheek with her cold fingers.

"I took us here so we could be alone, and talk, without disturbance. I've badly wanted to do so for a very long time." She turned away and climbed down from the coach. He watched as she tied the reins loosely on a branch, his breath coming fast. She looked up expectantly at him, and he too dismounted.

She had frightened him, an unfamiliar and unwelcome emotion. He looked at her, again seeing Angéla so clearly it tightened his craw. Erzsébet took him by the hand and kissed him. At first he was too stunned to move, then relaxed, allowing her tongue to press into his mouth. She pulled away and turned to the thicket.

She walked towards the grove, and after a pause, he hurried after her, glancing back at the abandoned carriage. The very real possibility of bandits in the wood worried at his increasingly-nervous mind but he pushed the thought away. He caught up to her and looped his arm around hers. She grinned up at him, but it failed to inspire the same warmth as before.

"Angéla told me all about you," Erzsébet said, ducking

under a low-hanging branch. "All about you."

He remembered how twice a month the sisters would meet for tea, usually the twinned visits within a few days of one other. He often wondered what they talked about, alone in their family estate.

"What did she tell you?" he asked, his mouth dry.

"Everything. We've always been very close. I felt I knew you, loved you, even, through what she told me."

He was silent, his heart clobbering the inside of his chest, skeletal branches scratching at his hair and arms. She led him by the hand along a winding path seen only by her, deeper into the thicket. His boots sunk into the soft loam as they walked, and no birds called in the fading light. He wanted to tell her they should return before it got dark, but was oddly hesitant to break the quiet of the forest.

"How much did you love her?" Erzsébet asked quietly, her back to him as she led the way.

"As much as I could," the Baron replied, still wary of her questioning.

"Do you like it here, husband?"

"Yes," the Baron lied, glancing at the gnarled boughs closing in around them. "It's . . . it's nice. Peaceful."

"Indeed," Erzsébet nodded. "Angéla and I came here often as girls. It's only a short ways from our manse."

"Really?" The Baron looked about for a familiar marker, but saw only the shadowy limbs, the silver sky.

"We loved the wood more than anything, and since our parents let us roam free once we were old enough, we found many secret places like this. All the days spent here, just she and I." Erzsébet sighed.

The Baron swallowed, and swallowed again when it didn't banish the unexpected lump in his throat. Erzsébet had spoken more to him tonight than in all their other courtings combined, but rather than putting him at ease, this troubled him. The Baron began to suspect she might be just as strange as her sister.

"Do you like stories?" she had turned to him, her lips still curled in that queer smile.

"Yes, I suppose."

"Then I wish to tell you one, though you've heard most of it before." The more he stared at it the more her smile seemed of ice, of frost, of chill, dead winter without a trace of warmth.

"Very well," The Baron looked nervously at the deepening shadows. "Shall we return to the coach, and on the way back we can—"

"No." Her voice was as cold as his ears in the autumn gloaming.

"But it will be dark soon, and we're leagues from home."

"Don't worry, there's time." She took his hand again, squeezing it softly. "My story begins ten years ago tonight, when the handsome, rich Baron took the poor yet comely daughter of his rival for a wife."

The Baron's stomach felt as twisted as the yew branches overhead.

"She was quite lovely," Erzsébet continued, "quiet and resourceful, and before she was wed she spent much time alone in this very wood, and of course, with her sister. The Baron financed a wonderful wedding, and the young girl's only regret was that she would be parted from her darling sister. But on the carriage ride back to his keep after the ceremony, he promised she would be allowed to visit her sister as often as she liked. So all was splendid for the young couple, and it is hard to say if she had more love for him or he for her, so deeply did they care for one another."

Erzsébet's smile widened as she talked, but the Baron scarcely noticed. Her voice had bewitched him, sending him back through the years to when he and Angéla were both so happy. Despite the cold and the queerness of the setting, he returned her smile.

"Their wedding night was all that lovers dream of, with silk sheets and perfumed candles and a blazing hearth, so for the life of him the Baron could not fathom why when they were finished Angéla cried softly on his chest, her tears cold as a frozen pond. But in the morning they smiled at each other, and that first autumn and winter passed with many nights spent in the same bittersweet fashion. But then, in the spring of their first year together, things changed."

The Baron's smile faltered, than died on his lips.

"She did indeed tell you everything, I see," said the Baron, not wanting her to continue, "I hardly see the point in—"

"Don't interrupt," her eyes flashed at him like torchlight on a naked blade, and he let her go on.

"Was it her tears after they had lain together that bothered him so? Or was it the distant look in her eyes when she gazed out the window towards the wood, towards home? Or was it some hidden savagery of his own soul that grew stronger, subduing the other, kind half of his heart? I know not, as I doubt you do. But it is beyond question that things turned sour, as love often does when it begins so achingly sweet.

"She no longer aroused the same fire within him, and despite her eager efforts he became unable to consummate their love, no matter how hard she tried. He would scowl across the bed at her, sickened either with her or himself. The months passed, the giddy heat of summer invading the stone walls, and still, no progress. He began to think dark thoughts, especially when she left to visit her sister.

"And so, on the night of their first anniversary, when he was again unable to muster sufficient passion and she lay cuddled at his side, she begged him; if there was anything he wished from her, any carnal secret he dared not voice, that he act upon it, anything at all that would please his heart. The cold saltwater on his breast indeed stirred him as he had not been in many frustrated nights, and he took her.

"This time it was different. He bit at her, not the gentle nibbling of hares but the gnawing of wolves, he pulled her hair and spat, and as their moans grew, he struck her twice on either side of her face. This time when they were finished there were no tears, just her smile, her teeth shining in the dark.

"The following day the Baron could barely contain himself, and before the sun had set he dismissed the staff and again went to course, yet more violently than before. But no matter how hard his blows, even when her teeth went loose under his knuckle and her hair came loose between his fingers, no tears fell from her green eyes, and within a month the baron tired of this new game. As the year turned and the snows returned, he was as frustrated and impotent as before."

The Baron wished more than anything that she would stop, but he dared not disturb her. Erzsébet's eyes were wide as she spoke, as if the scene she described played out between the yew branches. Her chest heaved with excitement, and he envisioned Angéla whispering their most holy of secrets to this pretty young thing.

"She loved her husband as much as she despised herself, and in an effort to stir his passions she gave him a small dagger, and with trembling hands he delicately ran it over her skin. She squirmed with arousal, but he could not act upon his growing desire until he pressed gently with the knife, drawing a thin line of blood across her back. Then he was able.

"But as the weeks passed and every sheet in the house became stained with rusty streaks, the Baron again became useless. His desire grew and grew, however, maddening him. So he secretly went to work on a room, remodeling the chamber that would have served as a nursery had she born him a child."

All at once the chill of the air returned, settling into the Baron's bones, and he shivered under his cloak. No, he thought, she would not have, not the room. That was theirs, between he and her, not even her sister could know, he had instructed her. But then it would not be the first of Angéla's betrayals, he thought glumly.

"By day they occupied themselves with tasks and obligations, and each night the Baron left his wife asleep as he stole off to the nursery. All through the death of winter and the birth of spring he labored. Special items were imported in ebon boxes, crates shipped from all over the continent. He spent hours discussing custom pieces with the local smithy, who created works of iron and steel to his exact specifications. The spring passed, and still Angéla lay alone in their bed.

"Finally, as summer returned to the land, his room reached completion. He stared at his wife with dark eyes as he told her of it, and at her request, they went to the room. The moon weak and slender through the window, a fire burning in the hearth, Angéla saw the culmination of his work for the first time, and it took her breath away.

"A large stone slab filled the center of the room like a pagan alter, a small drain at the foot of it. From the walls hung metal contraptions and wooden devices more suited for a dungeon than a nursery. Her heart pounded as she turned unsteadily to her husband, and she reached for his hand. He pulled away, bolting the door. That evening was as passionate as their wedding night, and her tears mixed with the trickle of blood spiraling down the drain.

"As sunlight entered the room and the hearth grew cold, he unshackled her from the slab, allowing her to curl up against him, sobbing with eyes long since drained of moisture. And the Baron smiled, his affliction cured. He carried her back to their bedroom and draped her in blankets, then returned to the room. He lay on the cooling slab, and enjoyed the first peaceful sleep in many months.

"But when he awoke late in the evening and surveyed the ill-lit room, self-disgust bloomed in his heart. He stared in horror at the whips and blades, the chains and needles. He stared at the caked blood in the drain, and barely made it to the window before retching.

"As he gazed down at the darkening forest below, he felt a sudden compulsion, and realized what he must do. Putting his heel on the ledge, he made to leap out, ending her misery as well as his own. But then the door swung inward, for he had forgotten to bolt it.

"Angéla stood in the doorway, a platter in her hands. Their eyes met, and she smiled warmly. He turned back to the forest, and would have jumped had she not spoke.

"Are you a coward then, husband?" She asked, setting the tray on the slab. "Are you so afraid of me, of yourself, that you choose death over pain?"

He looked curiously at his wife. She walked to the wall, inspecting the apparatuses. Her words seemed mocking, without hesitation or doubt. The platter she had brought was stacked high with smoked meats and cheeses, and a flagon of wine. Angéla faced him from across the room, a small barbed crop resting in her palm.

"I've sent Paul and the rest home, so after you've eaten—" she trailed off, smiling that odd smile of hers.

"The Baron turned away from the window, his legs shaking. He went to the tray and tore into the venison, guzzling wine as he stared at his wife. She disrobed while he ate, her smooth skin marred with dozens of scabs, hundreds of scars. She handed him the crop as he finished, and as the moon rose over the trees, she began to scream."

The Baron could hardly breathe, and staring at Erzsébet, he longed for the absent veil so she wouldn't remind him so of her sister.

"She showed me those scars, those wounds, let me trace them with my fingers as she told me how each mark was laid upon her. And despite my fear I longed to see this room, to feel the indescribable sensations you gave her, to know the passion she found in such exquisite pain. But forgive, I am digressing.

"Years passed. Often they would have to wait a week or even a month for Angéla to recover enough to return to the chamber. They rarely spoke anymore, and the Baron was secretly pleased that she remained without child. But then, as their fourth anniversary came and went, he began to grow suspicious of her silences, of her walks alone in the wood.

"He found significance where there was none, imagining she kept a secret lover, and this enraged him, though he had no proof. He suspected the visits to see her sister were actually to meet another man, to cuckold him under his very nose, and so he stopped allowing her to travel, instead having me visit her at his keep. But while we both knew you had become fiercer in your debaucheries, more demanding in your desires, neither of us dreamed you would murder her."

The Baron coughed, forcing his shaking body to take air. Sweat oozed from him, and he stared with revulsion at Erzsébet. This was too much. He looked around, expecting men to emerge from the trees. Could her motive in bringing him to the desolate woodland be revenge after all?

"And now I must confess, husband, a secret known only to my sister and I," Erzsébet's smile seemed at his expense, dark and mischievous. "I've lain with you before, dear Baron, many, many times."

The Baron felt light-headed, almost drunk.

"I craved the sensations just as Angéla needed to escape them at times, so that before the room was even built, I would return in her place when she visited, sharing your table and your bed. I would spend a few days with you, while she took my place at home."

"Balderdash!" The Baron spluttered, his mind reeling at the suggestion. "I would have noticed, I would. You couldn't, I made her unique, I would have known!"

"Would you?" Erzsébet chuckled. "Alone in our room, and later, in your bedroom, when we met each month we would study her body, cataloging each lash and cut. Then, just as you gave them to her, she would give them to me. Sometimes I would have to feign exhaustion if a scar was too fresh, lest you notice the difference. And you grew to suspect her of adultery, while all the while it was you who lay with another!" Erzsébet laughed, her voice echoing through the thicket.

"No," the Baron shook his head and sat down hard on the ground. "No."

"Yes." Erzsébet shifted about, loosening her straps and buttons. There was a rustling, and through the gloom the Baron saw her step from the heap of clothes. Just like her sister, she obviously eschewed the more complex and constraining undergarments which plague the fairer sex. And true to her word, her supple form was pitted and scarred, her breasts striped red, her stomach and thighs cross-hatched with purple and gray lines. Her body was identical to Angéla's, every mark and wound replicated perfectly, save those last gifts he had given her . . . .

"And while you never knew what was going on, you sensed something was amiss, that she snuck off without you ever catching her. So you punished her, you punished her as much as you could. You killed her, because you thought she was unfaithful."

"No," the Baron fought back tears, doubt and guilt long submerged rising in him like a storm-drunk river. "An accident, that's all, an accident—"

"An accident?" Erzsébet's eyes seemed yellow in the dusk. "An accident? Yes, I suppose it must have been. An accident you riddled her breasts with skewers, an accident you defiled her with brands, an accident you flayed her back until the skin hung in bloody clumps like the broken wings of a fallen angel. An accident that when she begged for death you kept her alive, letting her suffer as the moon rose and fell and the wolves bayed. An accident, was it?"

"Yes!" the Baron blubbered, tears blinding him. "No, I . . . I didn't know, I'm sorry, I . . . I made a mistake."

"I'll tell you another story, a short one." Erzsébet walked away from him, the branches wrapping around her like a cloak. "When I was coming of age to wed, I wished more than anything to avoid it all, to live in the wood with my sister and never return to my family home. I loved the smells of the forest, the beasts that lived there, the feel of grass and dirt under my naked back. And once, when my sister was bedridden with fever and I wandered here alone, I met a man in the wood. At first he scared me, for he was tall and strange, dressed all in yellow; but he harkened me, and seemed broadminded, friendly and inclined to listen.

"So we talked. I told him of my love for the wood, and he nodded in agreement. He seemed to be a worldly gentleman, and he told me of a way I might achieve my desires, as farfetched as they might seem. He told me how I could cast off the shackles of my station, and those even more physical bonds. The path would be long and hard, but if I did exactly as he instructed I could remain in the wilds forever.

"So I accepted his offer despite the harshness of the terms. I wrote my name in his book, and from that day forward once a month I would go alone into the forest, forcing my sister to keep inside with the doors bolted. And when the moon rose I felt myself change, the conversion accompanied by a pain unlike anything you could bestow upon me. And after the suffering I would be free throughout the night, to smell the creatures and plants, to hunt and run and croon.

"My heart was always heavy in the morning when I returned to my old self and my old home, only my sister knowing my secret. The man in yellow had told me how I could stay that way forever instead of one night every thirty, but his terms seemed impossible. Until I met you."

"What?" The Baron had stopped crying, gaping up at Erzsébet.

"I dared not simply sneak off every month lest you notice my absence, and since my poor naïve sister was as eager to experience the embrace of a man as she was to help me hide my condition, we engineered to trade places twice each month, so you wouldn't suspect. But suspect you did, and you killed her, the only good and innocent creature I've known save those in the fields and forests. Poor, poor Erzsébet, dead because she sought to please both you and I."

The Baron tried to speak but his tongue wouldn't obey. Angéla towered over him, her naked body glistening with sweat. She looked down at him with contempt.

"I paced all night outside the walls, listening to her screams and your laughter. In the morning while you slept I crept back inside the keep for the last time and beheld what you had done to her. I could smell her fear stagnating in the room, and your sweat, your piss. In a rage I almost went to you sleeping on the slab, to open you up with your own knives, to let you cower and plead as she had. But I remembered too well the deal I had made in the wood, so instead I slunk away, back through the forest to my family manse. I feigned illness to account for my haggard condition and frenzied sorrow the first few days home, and as my parents have always been distracted and easy to please the ruse went into place effortlessly. Then came the news that Angéla had fallen from the ramparts of your keep, and Erzsébet was an only child.

"Do you know why I wept that first night we spent together and so many after? Because at first I thought you were a kind man, and I knew to fulfill the bargain I must one day kill you, and I hated myself for it. Then later, I thought it was somehow my fault that you couldn't take me, and when you built the room I cried tears of joy, for I felt wicked and terrible and I craved your punishment for my deception, for my intentions. But now I see you for what you truly are: a vicious and hurtful fiend, wicked in a way unknown to even the most brutish animal."

"Angéla," the Baron said, clambering unsteadily up from his seat in the loam. "Don't. Whatever you're planning to do, I beg you—"

"Beg? Like Erzsébet begged when you violated her beyond recognition? I blame myself for marking her to resemble me, but it was her idea, and I was not the one who killed her. Now fulfilling the bargain will be easy, much easier than convincing Father to let his darling Erzsébet marry the wealthy Baron despite the bad end Angéla came to. Do you know why we're here now, husband, in this grove so many leagues from any house or hearth?"

The Baron shook his head, too rattled to speak. The full moon had risen behind her head like a crown, shining into his eyes. All the old legends of witches and devil-worshippers flitted through his mind, denying him the ability to rationalize what had become of them both.

"I took you here because this is where I met the man in yellow, and this is where the pact was to be consummated. He gave me the endowment to change once a month, saying if I wished to fully enjoy the blessing, to run as beast under sun and moon without ever returning to my old form, I must wed. I must marry a man and keep my husband for ten years without his knowing my secret, and on the eve of our tenth year as man and wife, I must lead him out to this very thicket and here—"

"No!" The Baron bellowed, tackling Angéla. He drove her

into the spongy dirt, pinning her bare arms under his knees. He pummeled her face, harder than he ever had before, but only succeeded in slicing his knuckles on her hard teeth. He felt her stomach heave and pulse under his thighs, and scrambling to his feet, saw she grew three extra pairs of breasts along her stomach, the eight black nubs long and hard in the night air. Angéla's yellow eyes flashed, her smile wider than ever.

He fled as best he could through the trees, stumbling and tripping and getting caught up where the woven branches barred his way. Through the shadows he saw the carriage in a patch of moonlight, but as he pushed through the undergrowth the horses whinnied and stamped, jerking at their tether. The branch they were tied to snapped and the horses ran, the empty coach bouncing along behind.

The exhausted Baron slumped to the ground against a tree, tears running off his chin. He heard a throaty growling from behind but did not turn, closing his eyes and waiting for the jaws to close on his neck. Instead warm teeth sunk deep into his left palm, bones crunching, blood welling out.

The Baron screamed as he was dragged by his mangled hand back into the grove, too shocked to strike at the muzzle that gripped him. And throughout the night he waited for the bloody maw to seize his throat, but instead the she-wolf nipped away at his arms and legs, his stomach and more tender places still, slowly eating him alive as the moon rose higher into the dark branches. Watching the steam rise from the whimpering Baron, the man in yellow stepped from behind an ancient yew and grimly made to keep his side of the bargain.

Forest of Anguish

Sean Frasier

Things here got a nasty habit of not staying dead.

So reads the warning written in long dried blood on the cellar wall above a well-worn wooden workbench.

Don't get me wrong. I appreciate the thought—though it would've been nice if the notice had been posted somewhere I might have seen it *before* a skinless dog chased me into this old cabin, *before* I fell through a set of rotten floorboards, and *absolutely before* I found myself impaled by eight feet of rusted pipe.

A curl of slippery intestines dangles from the pipe like a spiral of party popper confetti as my own draining blood warms my back against the cold soil. The black cord from my Walkman leads to a set of headphones, silent beside my head. Inside the Walkman, an unmarked cassette with Johan's new riffs.

After the utterly forgettable, scowling, cross-armed practice space photo on our eponymous EP, the vote to come out to the Adirondacks to find a fitting rustic backdrop for our new doom opus *Forest of Anguish* was unanimous. So earlier in the day I drove out beyond the ancient gazebo where we used to make apple bongs in the *Eternal Malice* demo days and sped deeper into a sparsely populated county once famous for hot springs that smelled of sulfur.

I always considered punctuality one of my best attributes. Before each show you'd find me waiting outside the venue with my stacked toms when the other dudes finally roll up in our soccer mom van with Stonegoat stenciled on the hood, smoke puffing out of the sliding doors.

Here I am, first to arrive again, and this is where it gets me—anchored to this pole rammed through my stomach.

Anyway, rumors of the sulfur water's magical healing powers spread. Springs of eternal youth, the whole shebang. Nomadic con men came to bottle the water and sell it town to town a century ago.

Headache? Bum leg? Unfortunate growth on your genitals?

The cure for all that and more, right in this here bottle!

Of course, in the end it proved a cure for nothing save dehydration, the crippled awaiting miracles that never came, limping away and leaving behind yet another cluster of towns built on lies and a state park with an amphitheater where fuckin' Dave Mathews plays each summer.

It's a mania that sounds crazy to modern ears, sure—but I'd trade my last blunt right about now for a bucket of that water and a little bit of hope.

The dog peers over the edge of the hole, wet muscles and ligaments gleaming like something that recently escaped a butcher's shop display. Without skin or fur I can't tell the breed—except this was no lapdog.

I was always a cat guy anyway.

I try to muster a voice to shout for help, maybe frighten

away the improbable creature above me. All that comes out is a dry wheeze. I push my hands into my pockets. No cell phone, of course. Must have clattered away when I landed.

Murphy's Law: when things are fucked, they are seriously, tragically, supernaturally fucked.

I look back up. The dog is gone.

I consider my options: One, climb my way up the eight-foot tall pipe and push my body off it. Two, tear the pipe completely through my side. Three, lay here and die without all the fuss.

I deliberate between these uninspiring choices until I spot a rusted saw sticking out from the shaded space beneath the old workbench.

Maybe I could saw the pipe right above my belly and push myself over the top?

The dog whimpers up in the dim room above. I struggle and stretch towards the serrated blade. The pain as flaky, rusty metal scrapes against my innards is more epic than the *Forest of Anguish* opening track, but I'm making progress, stretching the hole in my stomach, extending my reach . . . .

And then the soil starts to move. A finger pokes out of the dirt, its nail frayed like old cloth. I see a faint twitch of darker blackness in the unlit expanse of the basement, something purposely remaining unseen. I listen for breathing and instead hear the wet shuffle of eyelids.

A full hand bursts from the tiny hole in the dirt, skin hanging from dirty bones, gray mud wedged in the joints. I yank my arm back. The hand scratches through the dust and black mulch, uncovering the handle of a hunting knife. It stabs the blade into the ground, using the leverage to pull its body up from layers of soil and centipedes.

Panic sets in.

I chop at the pipe with my hand like a drunken martial artist. A reeking mess of torn flesh draped like cobwebs from its limbs climbs from the earth.

The skinless dog dives from the gaping ceiling. A deep growl rumbles from its throat, decaying teeth snapping, wide lidless eyes glaring. I cover my eyes and wait for the end to come from one direction or another. The sound of skin tearing is like peeling cheap adhesive from a wall, but I feel no new pain. Peeking out through spread fingers I see the dog clench the skeletal hand in its mouth, chomping the dead skin of this unconventional chew toy to mush before flinging it into the mysteriously inhabited darkness, knife and all.

The dog nuzzles my face and licks the blood from behind my ear. I pet it cautiously, the muscles tough and slimy. I'm no expert of dog anatomy but, despite the rot, I'm gonna say this is a lady dog, based on the lack of protruding goods.

We had a dog growing up, for a year or so. Nothing special. Just a shitty, cranky, brown dog. One night we all went to sleep and when we awoke the next morning the dog house was empty.

First, we all pretended to be sad, said it wasn't right to replace him with another dog, bullshitted each other with the right words.

And then we got cats.

Whatever's in the darkness starts eating. I hear the sound of the anonymous monstrosity sucking the rancid meat right off the mangled hand. The dog snaps her teeth at the unlit corner, arches her back like she means business. A rotten stump of a wrist pokes through the hole in the ground and the dog snarls again, alternating threatening barks at the stump-occupied hole and the figure feasting in the darkness.

A dozen hands burst through the ground at once in a macabre synchronized swimming routine. The dog turns in a circle, growling at the ragged bodies rising from the ground. Wiry hair hangs over their faces, earthworms and earwigs creeping through the brittle strands. A dead child with ants crawling on his dried eyeballs crawls over to the dark pool of blood beneath me and lowers his mouth to drink. The dog pounces over me and knocks the child backwards.

It's official: time to revise my opinion of the canine species.

"Would you rather be eaten alive or burned alive?" our vocalist Magnus once asked me.

"Burned," I replied.

He'd spent the next twenty minutes passionately explaining why I was wrong, but I'd stuck to my guns, insisting I wanted to leave remains, even if it was just ash.

"Oh you'd still leave remains," Magnus clarified, "they'd just be in the form of your devourer's runny shit."

Of all the moments for this snippet of past conversation to pop into my head, this had to be the least opportune.

The corpses sneak to the bloody soil each time the dog turns, lifting the sludgy red dirt to their split lips. I push back at them weakly and gaze longingly at the saw beneath the workbench. I grab the dog's slippery muzzle. Her breath stinks like the goo lurking at the bottom of a slaughterhouse dumpster, but she gives my hand a reassuring lap. I direct her vision to the saw.

"Go get it, girl!"

She darts to the workbench, hurries back, and . . . drops a saliva-slick cell phone into my hand.

The saw still sits over in the shade. I guess no one ever specifically trained her for rusted saw retrieval.

A hiss comes from the blackness. The undead all stop and retreat to the safety of their opened graves.

Crowned by sunlight oozing from the wounded ceiling, dressed in a patchwork cloak of furs and leaves with a hood throwing shadows over its face, a slender seven-foot figure steps forward. Long fingers boasting nails like upholstery needles extend from the cloak. The dog whimpers and huddles close to me as the figure stares down at us from beneath a headdress of teeth and bones. Faint white specks of light sit in its hidden eyes—the only details I can discern besides the curling horns.

I give the dog a comforting pat on its skinless head and . . . .

Actually, enough of this "dog" shit. I'm naming her Dorrian. She looks like she'd be a Cathedral fan.

The corpses reach out and massage my scalp, parroting my actions, tousling my hair with ripped palms and broken fingers. Dorrian cuddles closer. The figure holds the knife Dorrian flung into the darkness, tapping its long fingernails on the handle as it leans closer. I smell grave moss and dried flowers.

It's sort of pleasant. I'd buy incense sticks with "grave moss and impending doom" on the label. Could even sell them at the Stonegoat merch table.

The cloaked nightmare steps forward. I pull up Johan's phone number and dial. Straight to voicemail. He probably knows they're running late and doesn't wanna hear me bitch.

"Johan, it's me. Don't come to the woods. I'm in trouble, man, just send help but *stay away*."

The figure reaches forward, gently plucks the phone away while I'm still talking and brings it to its hidden mouth. The curdled smell of refrigerator mold and sunbaked roadkill wafts my way.

I click on the Walkman, put on the headphones, and watch the wheels hypnotically turn.

Listening to Johan's new riffs is like watching mountains form in a time lapse—gritty, monolithic, throwing shadows a thousand miles long. It's his best work yet. I wonder if my disappearance is all they need to take off. A touch of tragedy on the press release, a benefit show to raise funds for the continuing search parties. Weedeater could headline.

Maybe *Forest of Anguish* will be the real remains I leave behind. I remember my stiff fill in the second bridge of "Midnight Suffering," shake my head. Doesn't matter. During shows I was just a sweaty blur of drumsticks and feral hair. Now I'll be the mysteriously departed drummer of Stonegoat, and pink-eyed heshers will blaze up in parking lots outside of DIY metal shows and theorize what happened to me for years.

Dorrian nuzzles my face. Moss and flowers. The knife lowers. I close my eyes as the guitars fade to silence. The cassette clicks off. Everything's warm. Everything's dark.

Sometimes it doesn't matter what legacy you leave, as long as you leave one.

1988 Behind the 9:30 Club

Tim Deal

Sully insisted on including a Farfisa organ on the record. He was a fan of the Fleshtones, and I could see our band edging closer to that sound. *Fleshtones vs. Reality* had come out the year before, and Sully was transformed. It wasn't my vision, and as far as I could tell, Jack, the drummer, wasn't into it either. I wanted things to develop organically, to grow into our own sound. Still, Sully had convinced us to road-trip to the 9:30 Club in DC to catch the band on tour. He fronted the money for the cover charge, borrowed his roommate's forest green Delta 88, and loaded it with malt liquor.

We left Fayetteville at three o'clock and didn't stop to piss until we hit Richmond. By the time we passed through Fredericksburg, the sun hung low in the sky and the three of us were already a little rocked. We threw the empties out of the window as we drove, aiming for mailboxes and street signs.

By dusk, the lights of DC lit up the horizon. We had listened to Sully's worn out Fleshtones cassette four times by then. Jack had passed out in the back seat after shouting out a fifteen-minute rant on Reagan and Iran-Contra over the din of the music. Once in the city, we passed in awe at the surreality of the Washington Monument, massive, glowing, and thrust into the darkening sky.

"Fuuuuck," was all I could manage.

Sully reached for his Fleshtones cassette and I stopped him with a deadly glare.

Parking was a pain in the ass in downtown DC, and the broken windows and graffiti were a far cry from the Mall and its pristine monuments and museums. We tried to rouse Jack, but he was down for the count, so we cracked the windows an inch and locked the doors.

It was nine-fifteen, and Sully speed-walked to the 9:30 entrance.

"All we've missed is the shitty opener," I said.

"The Pixies were once a shitty opener," he said over his shoulder.

We got to the door and I could hear an up-tempo ska-like scratch on a heavily distorted guitar. There was no organ, no telltale Fleshtones harmonica.

"They haven't even gone on yet," said Sully as he paid our cover. But I recognized the band the moment Ian Mackaye belted out the opening lyrics to "Merchandise." I didn't have the heart to tell Sully. This was no opening act, this was DC's own Fugazi.

He realized something was amiss when he got in and saw the crowd. This was not a Fleshtones crowd. It was the yet-to-be defined crowd of the post-hardcore movement—a mix of painted leather jackets and eight-eyelet Docs with torn flannel, Levis, and Chuck Taylors.

He gave me a look and I shrugged. "Beer," I said and squeezed into the bar to order four PBR tall boys. The bartender, a young mohawked girl in a DRI T-shirt, handed me the beers hanging from the plastic six-pack rings.

"Are the Fleshtones playing tonight?" I said.

She shook her head, "No that was last night."

I found Sully, deflated, in the back on one of the ratty couches.

"Fuck me," he said.

"Dude, sorry, but it's still Fugazi!"

"How did I get the dates wrong?" He popped open a beer and sucked it back. "I'm just not a Fugazi guy."

"Look we're here at the 9:30 Club, a fucking institution."

He shrugged.

Fuck it, I thought, and pounded the first PBR. I pulled myself away from the sullen cloud that had begun to form around Sully. It was a good crowd—alive, eclectic—and Fugazi cultivated a sound that was difficult to categorize. There were elements of hardcore, but also a rhythm that pulled from its funk and ska roots. It was Mackaye's distinct vocal style that did it for me. It was a departure from his rapid-fire lyrical assaults in Minor Threat, but it was still uniquely Mackaye.

And then there were the girls—shaved heads, pierced noses, tattoos, thick black eyeliner. I could only watch, as the music was too loud to try to approach and talk. In the meantime two beers turned into four, then six, then two shots of Wild Turkey, or maybe three. The band was nine songs in before they played "Waiting Room," and though I'd been psyched to hear it, I needed air, and I needed it bad. I walked out the first door I saw and found myself in an alley behind the club. The air was muggy and stale and I could smell the dumpster and the rotten run-off of whatever greasy spoons spilled out onto the bricks.

The world shifted. My equilibrium was for shit and I hugged the 9:30 wall to remain standing. I concluded that standing was overrated and instead slid down the bricks until I sat amongst the cigarette butts and coagulated pools of god knows what. I felt the bass line throb through the bricks and shook my head to clear it. "Waiting Room" was all about that bass line and I was missing it. I planted my feet, pressed my back against the wall and tried to stand. I got halfway up then tilted to the right, staggered, then fell hard to the pavement—my skull screamed with pain and I saw a flash of orange light before everything went black.

I woke up and it couldn't have been long because "Waiting Room" was just finishing to a round of applause and cheers. As the band announced "this is 'Break In,'" I heard a voice say "get the fuck back!" followed by the smash of glass. I opened up one eye and tried to lift my head. It throbbed, my stomach lurched, and I threw up.

"Oh my God are you all right?"

I spat and tried to answer but it came out as "ffleggine"

I turned and scooted up the wall until I was sitting. My right eye didn't want to open, but from my left I spied a figure to my side, brightly adorned, and poised as if in mid-action.

Smash! She let loose another bottle, which exploded near one of the overladen green dumpsters.

"What the fuck?" I managed.

"Rats," she said.

"Rats?" but then I saw them—huge, mottled, beefy things with leathery gray tails. They were scattering after the bottle hit, but then immediately began to slow, turn, and reassemble into small groups. There had to have been about ten or twelve of them.

"I'm Amber," she said. "This is my first 9:30 show."

I turned and sharp pain spiked in my head. She was young, I'd say no more than seventeen, wearing light blue acid washed jeans, a pink shirt with ruffled shoulders, and a clean white pair of Keds.

Fucking Keds.

A total fucking *Betty*—bow and everything. It held her full blond hair from a face that was gleaming with toothpaste commercial vitality.

"I'm, uh, Marcus," I said. "And I'm fucked up."

"I saw you in the club," she said. "I wanted to come talk to you but it was too loud. Your head looks bad. You're bleeding."

I brought my hand up to my head and felt stickiness. More than I had expected, but nothing critical. I needed to go. Where the fuck was Sully? Was he not curious at all about what happened to me? My head swam. I could barely sit up let alone walk. I glanced again at the rats. I thought there had been ten or twelve, but the shadows beneath the dumpster seemed to teem with them. Their tiny eyes reflected the pale light that hung—just barely—outside the 9:30 door. A shiver went down my spine. I looked back to Amber. She had collected a small arsenal of beer bottles, which were arrayed around her crossed legs. A plastic grocery bag sat tied by her left knee.

"I tried to make it to the Divinyls last week, but I couldn't get out of a cheerleading fundraising event. My squad is trying to buy a Guatemalan kid a new kidney."

"Cheerleading?" I said.

"Yeah," she said. "Go Cubs! Um, we have a white one and a gold one."

"A white and gold what?"

"Tiger cubs. Aren't you from DC?"

"No, Bragg, North Carolina."

"As in *Fort* Bragg?"

"Yeah, look, I need to find my friend."

"Your friend? The guy you walked in with? Oh he left."

"Sully? You're sure?"

"Totally—hold that thought." She hucked another bottle, it smashed, I winced, the rats scattered. "Yeah, he left like five minutes after you came out here."

"I'm fucked," I said. "He was my ride. I live five hours from here."

"Georgetown Visitation Prep is the only school on the Eastern seaboard to have two mascots—tiger cubs, one white and one gold."

I managed to get my right eye open to a squint, but all it gave me was an indistinct fuzziness through the blood that had caked in my lashes. My stomach lurched again, but I swallowed it down. I wanted so desperately to sleep it off.

"I've got to see if Sully waited for me. I've got to get to the car."

"Of course," she said. "Can you stand? Can I help you?"

She stood, took my hand, and pulled. I tried to get up, almost got there, then her hand softened and I crashed back down against the wall—whirling bright bottle rockets of pain.

"What the fuck?"

"I'm sorry, you're too heavy for me. My hand slipped."

Smash! Another bottle.

"Why are there so many rats?" I said.

"I ask that question a lot."

I could hear the music give way to applause. More stage chatter, and I guessed the band was going on a break. For some reason I'd hoped that more people would wander out the back door and join us. Meanwhile, the rats had begun to assemble beneath the dumpster again, their wet noses glistened in the light. They tentatively moved toward us and I waited for Amber to throw another bottle. Nothing. I looked at her, she looked at me.

"The rats," I said.

She smiled, picked up another bottle, and absently tossed it in the direction of the dumpster.

"I think you know my sister," she said.

I most definitely did *not* know her sister.

"I think you, uh, must be mistaken," I said. "I don't hang out here."

She gave a quick glance at the rats and I followed her gaze. There were more now, and they no longer hid in the shadows. Her gaze shifted back to me.

"Weren't you at the Social Decision show?"

"Social *Distortion*?"

The rats had begun to creep forward again and I was shocked and bewildered to see so many. It was an army of rats, twenty to thirty of them. Big ones.

"That's what I said."

"The rats?" I said and nodded towards them.

"Yeah," she said. "The rats. My sister was at the Social . . . *Distortion* show. I think it was two months ago. She met a guy, a punker like you, and—"

"A *punker*?" I said. "I'm not a punker, I'm just a guy."

"Okay, so she met a *guy* like you. He asked her out here to 'talk.' My dad got a call at four the next morning. It was DC

Metro. They said that Krista was in the hospital, that she had been raped and beaten. She had been left unconscious, and she had lay out here for hours until someone had found her."

"That's terrible. I'm sorry. What does this have to do with me?"

She had picked up the plastic bag and begun to untie it.

"The attack had already left her emotionally and physically battered, but then the rats came. My sister may not have looked like everyone else. She may have pissed my parents off with the way she dressed, the music she listened to, and the guys she hung out with, but she was still my sister. She fucking hated cheerleading, but she never ragged on me about it."

The rats were halfway between the dumpster and us. I felt pretty sure I could get up and get out of there, but then a wave of nausea swept over me.

"The rats," I said again, and nodded towards the bloated vermin that crept towards us.

Amber picked up a bottle, but she didn't throw it. She pointed it towards me as she talked.

"When they found her, her fingertips had been chewed off. Her nose had been eaten through to the cartilage. And you know what really upset her? You know what made her break down to our dad and cry? The fact that she had missed her curfew."

"Fuck, that's horrible," I said then dry-heaved for a few seconds. When my stomach settled I looked at her, really tried to connect. "I saw Social-D at the Cat's Cradle in Chapel Hill last week. I wasn't at the 9:30 Club show. I haven't been here since Gang Green played, since Bad Brains and Bad Religion. I don't know your sister, and I am so sorry about what happened to her, but—"

Amber had opened the bag. She was careful not to spill its

contents on her jeans or blouse. She pulled it open with dainty, glitter-painted fingernails. There wasn't an ounce of malice in her disposition when she poured its contents on my lap— a pungent stew of rotted meat and vegetables, bones, fat, and gristle. The stench rose up and gagged me, and as I tried to stand, Amber took the bottle in her hand and smashed it against my forehead.

I didn't black out, but I was stunned enough to sit back down, and that's all the time it took. The rats, spurred on by the scent of garbage, came at me without hesitation. They devoured the garbage within minutes, and just before the scream erupted from my lips, Amber had this to say:

"Maybe it wasn't you. I get that, and in a way, I'm sorry . . . "

She was as mainstream as they come, but there was no denying her beautiful blue eyes and perfect blonde hair. She was the kind of girl that would not have given me the time of day in high school. And while I screamed and scrambled away from the hungry bloated rodents that went at me, she stood there with an odd look on her face—something like fear, disgust, and regret all rolled up into one.

"I'm truly sorry," she said. "But that doesn't matter right now, does it?"

I pushed them off of me. I fought and kicked and crawled.

Fugazi started into "Glue Man" as I struggled beneath the weight. I wondered if anyone had any idea about what was happening out here.

Amber turned and walked away, but I didn't call out to her. I knew she wouldn't return.

What I Learned as a Groupie

Stephanie M. Wytovich

There was sex,
there was drugs, there was booze,
and I stood in the middle of it all
lip-syncing the words to the song they all sang,
and trust me, they all sang the same song,
and it was a tune I knew well, for I was a girl who knew
her way around the music scene, the metal scene, hell—maybe
I was just a girl who knew her way around—but I'd learned a
few things between the cocaine dreams and the cigarette burns,
the blackouts and the fights: a musician can tell you he loves
you, and maybe he thinks he does, but he'll always love being
on stage more,
always crave that mic stand in between his legs
rather than whatever is hiding in between your thighs,
and the screams from a full house—a packed house!—will
always sound better to him
than any sound you could make while on your back,
because you're a fan,

not a critic,
and in this industry,
everyone wants to be famous,
but everyone also likes to get fucked.

Odious

JR Hayes

Doom County is about ten miles south of Satan Springs, nestled in the desolate valley between Murderfield and Wasteland Acres. The weather here is either dreary and overcast or violent black hailstorms. I think maybe the sun came out once in the eighties.

You're probably wondering why I would live in such a place. It's a reasonable question. Here's the deal—I was spawned within the county limits, so an ancient curse prevents me from ever leaving. If you're from Toledo, or Galveston, or anywhere else, you may come and go as you please, but us natural born Doomers, well, we're here for the duration. It sounds a lot worse than it is. I mean, sure, it would be nice to fly to Cincinnati for the day or drive to Hartford for a long weekend, but alas, it's just not in the cards. I think it's important in life to stay focused on the positive. For instance, Doom County has the most graveyards of any county in the United States. Take that Crook County, Wyoming!

My name's Gary. I'm a ghoul. Most people aren't very

familiar with ghouls. We don't garner anywhere near the same amount of press as say, vampires or werewolves. Even mummies are more popular than ghouls, and let's be honest, mummies are freaking stupid. I think the big problem is that there are no celebrity ghouls. We don't have a Nosferatu or Frankenstein's Monster or Creature from the Black Lagoon. The world's most well known ghoul is probably former Attorney General Janet Reno. So, there you go.

Here's what you need to know about ghouls. We are low-level demons who rob graves and eat dead flesh. Not to be confused with zombies, who eat brains and pre-buried flesh. In fact, a zombie will eat pretty much anything if you smear a little blood on it. Ghouls, being smarter and more sophisticated than zombies, understand that human flesh is only good when it's been embalmed and buried for six-to-seven weeks, giving it the dank and earthy rottenness that you want. *Mmm-mmm.* I'm getting hungry just talking about it.

I realize some people out there might find what I do a little un-PC, and all I can say is, I'm a freakin' ghoul, okay? I was bred by the Dark Lord to rob graves and eat flesh, so that's what I do. Every single freakin' night. Well . . . that's not *entirely* true. Some nights I stay in and watch horror movies and drink root beer floats . . . but that's beside the point. My point is, these claws were created to dig into earth. My teeth were made to tear human flesh. I am possessed by the fires of Hell and the never-ending hatred of the Dark Lord himself, which occasionally compels me to commit heinous and despicable acts of torture and desecration.

Aside from that, I think I'm a pretty easygoing guy.

During the day I sweep the floor at Hex, the local magic

shop on Doom St. Warlocks have been known to cross dimensions in order to peruse their rare spellbooks and artifacts. Every item in here is at least 3,000 years old, so you can just imagine how much dust there is. That's where I come in. I've spent the last half hour trying to bag a haunted cobweb, and I'm just about at the end of my rope. I yell to my boss, Mrs. Dingleweed. "I'm taking a flesh break, Mrs. D!"

"That's fine, Gary. Just make sure you go around the side of the building so you don't gross out the customers."

I walk outside to my bike, grab my lunch from the basket on the handlebars. I drool a little bit as I peel back the tinfoil. Inside is a rotten hand and a dill pickle. Sometimes I'll rub in some Cajun spices and deep fry the hands—you know, just to shake things up a bit; but at the end of the day, there's really nothing like a regular old rotten hand, freshly dug up the night before. It's just a classic.

I'm gnawing the last bits of nail from the pinky finger—the best part—when I see Mr. Weasal running down the street, white with terror. He, like most of Hex's customers, is a wannabe wizard, a weekend warlock. Of the hundreds of people who might shop here on a given day, only a small handful are actual sorcerers, most are just con artists, dilettantes, or middle aged women looking for love potions—aisle seven, in case you were wondering. Mr. Weasal runs like a man possessed, pointy, star-covered hat pinned tightly to his head. He keeps saying, "She's coming!" over and over again.

Some other people on the street seem to understand what he means. They scurry around like roaches before fleeing in every direction except the one Mr. Weasal had come from.

Who could be so dangerous, so wicked, they could send the

entire neighborhood into such a frenzy?

Mr. Weasal enters Hex shouting at the top of his lungs. I watch through the front window while everyone runs for the exits as if the store were engulfed in flames. Mrs. Dingleweed trembles nervously behind her 9,000-year-old Atlantean cash register, obsessively wiping sweat from her bifocals. I've seen War Demons and Genocidal Spirits run amok in the spell section without her even batting an eye. What could spook her like that? Could the Dark Lord himself be coming here to shop? Perhaps I should run home and get my bowtie and suspenders? If the master is in town, I want to look spiffy.

Then I see a slim young woman coming down the street in a tattered black dress and veil. I can see her pale body glowing intermittently through her clothing, as if it were struggling to contain a dark and menacing energy. Trees and bushes recoil as she moves past. Even the fire hydrants and parking meters seem to lean away from her. She walks past me into the shop as if I wasn't even there, and after her follows a frigid and deathly chill, like someone walking over your grave.

Through the doorway, I watch her complete her transaction. It's all very quick and quiet. Mrs. Dingleweed moves faster and more efficiently than I ever thought possible. As the mysterious woman exits the store, some of the roofers working on the Crematory Depot hoot and catcall. She stops and slowly sets her gaze upon them, removing her veil. Her tangled black hair, infested with spiders, looks as if it's alive. Her face is very beautiful, by human standards anyway, which only serves to rile the men up all the more. The harassment intensifies.

Her eyes glow blood red. A wave of her hand and the whole street begins to shake. One of the roofers bends back like a horseshoe and begins eating his own leg—boot, pants, and all. Another shoots himself in the face with a nailgun, while a third takes a claw hammer to his own head. Enormous steel I-beams are wrenched apart and fused together in midair, forming a set of makeshift crosses.

In a bloody storm of rivets, she crucifies thirteen men.

Levitating them with her right hand, she levels the entire building with her left. Then spikes the steel crosses down into the rubble. It's totally rad.

She turns her glowing, murderous eyes to me.

Uh-oh.

We ghouls aren't helpless by any stretch. In fact, most humans wouldn't stand a chance against our razor sharp claws. In this moment, however, helpless is *precisely* how I feel. Her gaze is so intense that I can feel it physically upon me—like a blistering heat wave, full of sadness and loathing, agony and revenge. She could destroy me with a small gesture, but she doesn't. Instead she turns away and disperses into the ether like smoke.

Mrs. Dingleweed comes running up. "My goodness, Gary. I thought she was going to disintegrate you."

"Yeah, me too," I say, breathing a sigh of relief. "Who the hell was that?"

She looks at me like I'm crazy. "You don't know who Diana the Despoiler is? The most foul and accursed witch in the whole county?"

"The lady that lives on Goblin Hill? That's her? How come I've never seen her before?"

"She only leaves the house very rarely." She looks across the street at the dusty ruins of Crematory Depot. "She's not much of a people person."

Police and firemen arrive, but there isn't much they can do other than stand around and admire her handiwork.

"What did she buy?"

"A couple of rare Egyptian torment spells and a bag of dark chocolate covered maggots." She looks at me with motherly concern. "You know, you should just forget about her right this instant. She spared you this time for some reason, but next time you won't be so lucky! Now get back to work, your break was over five minutes ago!"

Mrs. Dingleweed shoos me back into the store and I resume my sweeping. Still I can't seem to concentrate. All I can think about is the witch and her hypnotic gaze. I also feel strange physically. There's a wild thumping in my chest, an odd butterfly feeling in my stomach, and I kind of feel like I want to dance, which is a first for me.

Maybe I'm just hungry.

Later that night, as I sit upon a tombstone, tearing the rotten meat from a forearm, I still can't seem to shake the witch's face from my mind. No matter how many bodies I dig up, no matter how much dead flesh I eat, there is no satisfaction to be found. I am left empty, wanting, and most of all, deeply perplexed.

I wander home around two a.m. to the basement of the destroyed house in which I live. There's a front door, no roof, not much of a back wall. My roommates and I have laid down some steel plates to help protect the basement from Doom County's perilous weather, but sometimes, even steel plates are not enough.

Freddie is home, like always. Freddie is a fiend, which means he will eat anything he can get his hands on and requires constant aural and visual stimuli. Imagine a gorged tick the size of a VW Bug, a hundred mouths on his belly and a hundred eyes and ears on his head, ten thousand arms, most of them constantly feeding cheese curls to the mouths, others playing Gameboys or holding up smart phones and televisions for his many eyes to examine. He also listens to dozens of radio shows and albums simultaneously, at deafening volumes.

Freddie can be a very tough demon to share a basement with.

I open the fridge, and notice all my leftover feet are gone. I yell for Freddie. He doesn't hear me, of course. He never hears me. I go bang on his door until I have his attention.

"Hey, Gary. What's up?"

"Did you eat all of my leftovers, Freddie?"

"I thought they were gonna go bad."

"It's rotten flesh, Freddie. It doesn't go bad."

"Yeah, I guess you're right. Sorry, Gary, I'm a fiend and I guess it's just hard to control myself sometimes. You're not mad are you?"

"No, I guess not. Just don't let it happen again, okay?"

"You got it, buddy. How was work, by the way?"

"It was really crazy, actually. There was this witch . . . . "

"Wow, that's great, man. Hey listen, I'm kind of in the middle of something here. I'm trying to watch every episode of *Dawson's Creek* at the same time. So can you, you know . . . . "

"Oh, yeah. Sure, sorry. I'll just—" Freddie closes the door in my face. "—yeah."

This always happens—I go to his room angry about one thing and leave apologizing for something else. Oh well, he probably wouldn't know what I'm talking about anyway. I'll have to wait until Telly gets home from his haunting. He'll know what's wrong with me. Telly knows everything. In the meantime,

I eat some Vegemite, the only real substitute for rotten human flesh.

Telly comes through the ceiling around four a.m. He is the ghost of 70s television star/pop crooner Telly Savalas, best known for his role in the cop drama *Kojak*, as well as many feature films like *The Dirty Dozen* and *Cannonball Run II.* Telly is always dressed in an expensive suit and dark sunglasses, and has been smoking the same phantom cigar constantly for the last ten years. He's a super nice guy.

"Gary, baby, what's the matter? I've never seen you so out of sorts."

"I don't really know, Telly. There was this girl at work earlier . . . . "

"A girl, huh? Now you're speaking my language. Tell me everything about her."

Telly had a way of calming you with his smooth, deep voice.

"Well, she's a witch, and apparently very accursed, but also kind of pretty in a terrifying sort of way. She killed thirteen men and almost killed me. Now I can't stop thinking about her, and my guts feel all swirly. What's wrong with me, Telly?"

"Well, I don't know if it's the same for a ghoul as it is for a kid from New York, but it sounds to me like you're in love."

"In love? With a human? That's impossible."

"Maybe not as impossible as you think." He pats me on the shoulder. I can't feel it, but it's reassuring nonetheless. "Cheer up, Gary. Most demons never get to experience love. Hell, most humans don't either. You're actually very lucky."

"How could it be lucky to feel like this?"

"Well, sometimes love tears you up inside and makes you

want to die, but sometimes it makes you feel like you're flying, baby. It's the greatest feeling in the world."

"Really?"

"You betcha, kid."

"So, what do I do?"

"Well, for starters, you should tell her how you feel."

Goblin Hill is surrounded by a row of skulls on pikes, and it's peppered with twisted, burly sycamore trees. Her house is a small one-story cottage made of human bones. I'm dressed in my finest bowtie and suspenders. Telly told me to bring some flowers, so I grabbed some from the graveyard on my way here. I knock tentatively.

She opens the door. Her eyes are still red, but without the death-glow.

"What do you want?"

"I . . . uh . . . was wondering if you . . . uh . . . might be interested in maybe doing some graverobbing later . . . and I . . . think I might be in love with you but I'm not really sure . . . . " She waves her hand and my voice goes silent. My mouth moves, but there's nothing coming out.

"Your foolishness amuses me, young ghoul. So I will let you off with a light maiming. Do not darken my door again." She waves her hand to my left, and says, "Boys . . . . " Undead confederate soldiers start crawling out of the earth, bayonets at the ready. They chase me off the property, stabbing me the entire way. It takes a lot to kill a ghoul, but they nearly succeed and that night, I do something ghouls never, ever do.

I cry.

Telly tries to console me, but I'm overcome with despair.

I have no idea what to do. He suggests picking up a love potion, but that would be like using handcuffs on Houdini. I'm doomed . . . .

Freddie peeks his hundred-eyed head around the corner. "What's his problem?"

"He's in love with a witch."

"Ha! Gary's in love! I'm totally gonna tell the Dark Lord."

"No, Freddie! Don't say anything, you big jerk!"

"Don't worry about him. He's just jealous. Fiends are jealous of anything they don't have."

"But what if he tells the Dark Lord? He'll rip me to shreds, he'll . . . . "

"Gary, baby, you think the Dark Lord has never lost his heart to a girl? You're crazy."

"The Dark Lord has been in love?"

"Oh yeah, a few different times. He still hasn't gotten over that fling with Ayn Rand, if you ask me." He passes me the Kleenex. "Here, blow your nose, clean yourself up, we're gonna get you out of the house."

"Where are we going?" I wipe my red, swollen face.

"The fair's in town."

I had completely forgotten about the Doom County Fair. This year there's supposed to be a wet witch contest, a fattest imp competition, daredevil unicyclists, skeeball, the Black Hole, the Tilt-A-Vomit, bumper planes, body bag toss, and, of course, barbed wire candy—a local favorite.

Freddie was trying to bankrupt himself at the World War VII shooting gallery, using ten laser rifles at the same time. You'd think it would improve his chances, but apparently not.

Telly and I watch some evil mimes for a bit. Unfortunately,

they're really lame, just like regular mimes. I consider taking back the quarter I had thrown into the hat, but decide that would be tacky. We walk past a dunk tank, where a mouthy troll starts making fun of my unibrow. I waste ten tickets trying to dunk that idiot. Then a little girl comes up right after me and nails it on the first try! Talk about embarrassing. Oh well, it's on to my favorite ride, Charles Manson's Subconscious! Scary stuff!

It's all fun and games for a little while, but eventually the accursed witch infiltrates my thoughts again.

Am I really in love? Or has she cast some diabolical spell upon me? I soon find myself as upset and discouraged as I was before we came. I attempt to drown my sorrows in delicious barbed wire candy, but even its sugary/painful deliciousness cannot cheer me up. Telly and I decide to leave. Freddie says he wants to hang around and get his picture taken with porn icon Ron Jeremy.

As Telly and I walk toward the exit, we stumble upon a bizarre device. The shape of it seems almost completely random, jutting out in every direction, a chaotic mixture of oak and rusty iron. There's a D-shaped door on one side, and two rickety antennas sticking out the top, with blue bolts flickering between them. This massive, homemade, technological monstrosity is precariously strapped to the bed of a tiny little Nissan truck. The door of the truck says "JIMBO'S SHAPESHIFTER" with a big thumb's up next to it.

Perhaps I can find another shape that pleases Diana more? Surely there has to be some form of life that she's fond of. Telly smells a con, but I won't allow myself to be talked out of it.

A round, hairy man wearing nothing but overalls approaches us. His mouth is so full of chewing tobacco that it's difficult to understand what he's saying.

"Howdy! I'm Jimbo."

"Nice to meet you, Jimbo. I'm Telly, and this is my friend, Gary. Does this machine really work?"

"I tell you what, my doohickey here'll shift yer shape fer ya can say 'Tennessee whiskey!'"

He tips his head back and howls like a coyote. Twice.

"Well, Mr. Jimbo. The thing is, I'm a ghoul, and I want to make sure that your machine will work on me."

"Do you have three tickets?"

"Well, yes."

He spits a glob the size of a tennis ball that lands with a loud splat. "Then my thingamajig gonna work on you just fine." He crams my tickets into his pocket, then quickly ushers me toward the entrance.

"What do I do when I get inside?"

"Well, on yer left yer gunna see a little white rat with some wires comin' out of his head. He's gonna ask ya, in yer brain, what ya wanna be, and all ya got ta do is think it, and there you'll be, just like that."

Inside, just like he says, the rat communicates with me telepathically. I try to think of something that a witch would like, and the first thing that pops into my head is a black kitten. Surely she wouldn't slay a defenseless kitten!

Telly's concerned that I might be stuck in kitten form permanently, but Jimbo says he'll be there all week, so I can change as many times as I want, provided I have the requisite number of tickets. I can keep changing until I find the perfect option. It's a foolproof plan, as long as she doesn't fry me with a lightning bolt or something.

The next day, I travel back to Goblin Hill and scratch at her front door for a while. She doesn't answer, so I jump off the windowsill, grab the knocker, and bang three times before tumbling back to the porch.

When she opens the door and sees me, she gasps in horror and quickly tries to back away, collapsing just inside the door, wheezing and breaking out in hives. She attempts to cast a few spells, but can't for whatever reason. I manage to dial 911 on her landline then run away.

I'm so scared that I killed her. I pray to the Dark Lord that she will be okay.

Telly and I go back to the fair and have Jimbo's machine turn me into an owl, so I can at least fly over and make sure she's alright. I think Telly feels bad for me, so he pays for the shapeshifting this time.

I fly to her house and watch her through her bedroom window. She seems fine physically, but also sad as she stares longingly at a photo of some woman.

Who could this woman be? A sister, maybe? An old friend?

I decide I better consult Telly.

Telly's theory is that she's a lesbian witch. He thinks I should shapeshift into a beautiful woman and attempt to seduce her.

I wasn't too sure about this particular plan, but I trust Telly. He would never knowingly steer me wrong.

It's also the last night of the fair, so it's kind of now or never.

The clouds turn a deep bruise. A black hailstorm is on the way. It starts coming down hard.

Jimbo's trying to close up shop, but Telly convinces him to let me give it a whirl.

This time, at the very moment the rat begins to speak to me through my thoughts, the machine is damaged by the giant hail. A series of malfunctions send sparks flying.

When the smoke clears, I'm still alive, but not entirely sure as what. I catch my reflection in a shard of glass.

Picture the furry body of a small possum, with spider legs on one side and cricket legs on the other, the head and pincers of a beetle, and the tail of a scorpion with a snake head instead of a stinger.

Telly keeps saying it isn't that bad, but I notice he's having trouble looking at me. Jimbo's device is totally destroyed, along with all hope of changing me back. Come to find out, since the shapeshift was done by a machine, magic could not undo it.

A word to the wise, always read the fine print.

I'm inconsolable. I ask Telly to drop me off at Diana's house. If I can't be with the woman I love, at least I can be squashed by her.

I crawl up to her door and let out a chilling chatter-hiss with my two mouths. Diana opens the door and looks down at me curiously. Then she sneers in revulsion.

"I declare, you are the most abhorrent, repugnant, revolting abomination I have ever seen . . . come here."

Diana bends down, scoops me up, and holds my new form in her outstretched arms, appraising me.

"I shall call you . . . *Odious*."

I chatter-hiss my approval.

She smiles, just barely, and it's sublime.

"Oh, you like that, do you?"

She takes me inside and I curl up in her lap on the couch. We watch *Return of the Living Dead* and eat dark chocolate covered maggots together.

Which are actually way tastier than you might think.

The Show Must Go On

John Palisano

"Don't look at my dick."

Andre and his longtime friend, Dave, stood next to one another at the crowded New Haven Coliseum men's room urinals.

"I said, stop trying to sneak a peek."Andre looked like Blackbeard, only without the beard. But that didn't mean Dave felt obligated to take his shit.

"Hell, you're the one wearing make-up like those chicks in Poison," Dave said, whipping back his long, straight, dishwater brown hair. He jiggled the last few drops, put his dong back in his jeans and made sure his ratty Sabbath shirt didn't get tucked in.

"They're poseurs, man," said another headbanger.

"No they're not," Andre said, tucking his junk all the way to one side of his zebra print spandex pants, just like David Lee Roth. "They're cool."

The debate was unwinnable. But doors had just opened. The house PA hadn't even kicked in yet. What else was there to do?

"I'll take Priest any day," Dave said, upping the ante. "Forget all this glam stuff."

"Halford's gay, dude," Andre replied. "At least you know Brett and C.C. are getting tons of ass. I mean, just listen to Priest's songs, dude. 'Breakin' the law' . . . the *sodomy* law. And he dresses like a leather queen. Look at their videos."

"Sacrilige, man," Dave said and combed his hair with an oversized white plastic comb. "You know not of which you speak. Doesn't matter. Priest's songs are better."

"Whatever. Just get me out of here. I don't want to miss Maiden. Let's—"

Buuuuuhhhh-racckkkkkk!

A squall of laughter swept through the dudes at this horrid sound echoing out from one of the stalls.

"Yo," Andre called. "Tailgaitin' a little too hard in the parking lot?" He turned to another guy at the sinks. "Remember last year when that kid got drunk and fell out of the top parking lot before the Ozzy show? People don't know how to drink anymore."

From inside the stall, a new, wretched sound filled the room.

"Guy sounds like he's in trouble," Dave said.

"Fuck 'im," Andre said. "Dumbass."

"Shut up, dude," Dave said, leaning down alongside the stall door. "I think this guy might be really fucked up."

He turned and looked at the stalls. He saw the guy's snakeskin boots underneath the door. They were spotted with little red spots, which, at first, he believed were just part of their design.

The sounds got worse. He inched closer and bent down.

"What are you doing? Trying to get a peak at that guy's peen, too, eh?" Andre wrinkled his nose.

"Shut up, dude," Dave said. "This guy's really fucked up." He pointed at the stall. "Hello? You okay in there?"

"Leave him alone," Andre said. "Just forget about it, man."

Blood misted down onto the snakeskin boots.

"What the . . . ?"

Before Dave could fully formulate a thought to express he backed away.

Andre turned, having heard the splashing, just in time to see a bucket-sized splash of blood fall to the ground.

Dave felt something moist on his head. He put his hand up to his scalp instinctively, took it away, and saw his hand smeared with blood. "Shit," he said.

He looked up to see where it had come from. There was a big bloody stain on the ceiling. As he spotted it, a stream of blood ejaculated from behind the stall, and hit in nearly the same spot. It splattered everyone within ten feet.

"Jesus," Andre said, his voice cracking. He thrust his hands into the nearest sink. "What the hell is this? Some kind of Alice Cooper thing?" Under the stall, a blood puddle expanded out past the stall doors, accompanied by the sound of sucking. Or munching, like the Blob, only grosser.

"Whoever's doing this," Andre said, "it's not fucking funny. This isn't a god-damned W.A.S.P. show."

"We need to get out of here," Andre made for the door. As he did, a heavy torrent of blood bounced off the ceiling and pegged him in back of the head, coating his hair, dripping down between his shoulder blades.

"This is bullshit!"

Andre returned to the sink and, cursing unintelligibly, pushed down five times on the towel dispenser. He spun both taps on full blast.

"Dude," Dave said quietly, "you look just like freakin' Sissy Spacek in that Stephen King movie."

"I don't give a fuck. I'm going to wash up, buy a T-shirt at the merch stand, and enjoy the show. That guy's an asshole, but this blood ain't real. It's not fucking funny. This isn't a goddamned W.A.S.P. show in here."

Dave looked at the other two guys. They'd all been covered in blood in a matter of seconds.

Dave didn't think it'd make a difference to wash up. In the mirror he caught sight of another spout of blood shoot out from behind the stall, bounce off the ceiling, drop and splash all over Andre's head. His arms, the paper towels and sink were all coated in red.

Andre roared. "Mother*fucker!*" He was not a happy headbanger.

"How can one person have so much blood in them?"

Dave looked around. Hadn't anyone else noticed or heard the noise? The security idiots were always on them, so why weren't they on them now when they needed them? They didn't care about metal fans. Nobody did. Except other metal fans.

The stall door crashed open. The first thing Dave saw was the back of a very tall dude dressed in black with real long, straight blond hair, kind of like Duff from Guns N' Roses or Robin Zander from Cheap Trick.

There was another guy sitting on the toilet, pants down, blood everywhere. Little sticky booger-shaped clots colored the stall.

The Blond Dude backed out.

Dave waved at the air in front of him. "He smells like shit."

Andre clenched his jaw. His face was coated in blood. "You stupid motherfucker. Look what you did to me."

He slapped a hand on the Blonde Dude's shoulder. "Listen, asshole. You're going to pay for this."

The Blonde Dude turned to face Andre. It didn't look like he had any lips. Andre could see bone through his cheek, for Christ's sake, right there, plain as anything. His eyes were all cloudy and blue. He had what looked like a hundred scratches all over his face and his eye sockets were sunken in so deep that he practically looked like a skull. That, and he looked hungry as all hell.

Andre took a swing, but Blond Dude turned in what seemed to be slow motion, intercepting Andre's knuckles with his mouth.

Blonde Dude bit down. Andre screamed, and not like Brett Michaels or even David Lee Roth on Van Halen's first album. No. He screamed like you'd think he'd scream: like a big old baby.

The unmistakable riff to Nugent's "Cat Scratch Fever" blared out the house PA. Blond Dude gnawed through finger and knuckle.When Andre finally managed to pull his hand away there was not much left other than a few wiggling flaps of skin.

Good thing I'm a singer, he thought. *I don't have to shred the guitar. Just sing. And I can wear a glove and no one will know.*

Blond Dude was on him again. Andre pushed back, but there was something unnatural about his attacker's strength. Andre found himself pinned between the exit door and Blonde Dude, blocking everyone else from fleeing.

Dave glanced over at what was left of the guy in the stall—

face down, head nearly chewed off, neck innards hanging out around his spine, skin on the edges white like when he used to cut worms in half in his front yard as a kid, furry, naked ass providing stark contrast to the blood and black matter all around. The water in the toilet bowl looked like someone threw up a whole case of fruit punch and threw in a couple of prunes.

That dude attacked that guy while he was taking a shit!

"Gross," one of the other headbangers said as if reading his mind,

They backed up, but only made it a step or two.

"Guys! Don't . . . leave . . . . "

Meanwhile, The Blond Dude was de-necking Andre one bloody starving zombie bite at a time. Trickles of flesh blood flowed freely from between the thing's teeth. Dave stood for a moment, not sure what to do.

I'm covered in blood, he thought. *They'll think* I *did something. Probably kill me.*

And while he was thinking that, the Blond Dude saw Dave out of the corner of his undead eye. Taking a break from his snack, the Blond Dude seemed to size Dave up with a look that said, *You're next for me.* Dave imagined what the Blond Dude thought. *Right after I get done with this one, you're next.*Dave didn't wait around another second. He turned and bolted, pushing past Blonde Dude to the exit. There was another exit, although it was shut. He pushed on the lever but it wouldn't budge. *Fuck*, he thought. He pushed again, imagining the Dude's hot breath on his neck.

Dave pressed his shoulder to the door and pressed hard. At last came a loud popping sound and he was out. The fuckers had locked the door. Big fire hazard. They didn't care about metal fans, anyway. Probably would love to have them all burn up in the bathroom of a show.

Dave was out. The door banged into the side of the hallway. He ran out into the hallway and standing smack dab in a throng of metal fans.

Halfway into the main concourse, people noticed he was covered in blood. Instead of running away in fear, or shock, or repulsion, Dave got nods and several thumbs up. "Hey," he said, at no one in particular. "There's something going on in the bathroom." His voice was cracking and he could barely compete with the PA, despite still being in the concourse.

"Metal, dude," someone said, and flashing him the devil horns sign.

"Who'd you kill?" another person said.

Two metal girls, dressed in animal prints and waist-pinching jeans, passed him and snickered. They said something, although he really couldn't hear what.

"Help," Dave said, his voice barely able to compete with the PA.

No one cared.

No one thought he was for real.

He scanned the concourse. A big, beefy Italian bouncer standing next to a ticket-taker caught his eye. Dave knew that'd be the guy to convince. He looked like he might be able to take down Blond Dude.

Maybe.

Dave forced his way through the crowd to the man.

"Hey," he said, panicked voice working at the top of his register. "There's something going on in the bathroom."

The bouncer ignored Dave at first—too busy using his

flashlight to undress a bouncy blond girl on her way into the show—but once he did notice him, he was not sympathetic.

Dave tapped him on the shoulder again. "Excuse me?" he said.

Finally, the bouncer looked at him. He took a second look, surprised at the blood covering the little pipsqueak bugging him. "What the hell's wrong with you?" he asked Dave then turned to the ticket-taker. "What the hell'd he put all over himself?"

"There's someone . . . there's been an attack."

"What?" The bouncer turned his flashlight to Dave—shined it right in his eyes. "You pulling my leg?" The bouncer's voice seemed to cut right through Ted Nugent's guitar. "Where?"

"Over there," Dave said, turned, and pointed at the Men's Room.

The Italian guy shook his head. "You're full of shit, you know that?" He turned halfway away from Dave. "I see. You're trying to get me to go in there so you guys can drop a bucket of whatever shit that is on you, on me, right?" His back was to Dave by the time he finished. "Get the fuck out of here before I throw you out."

The PA quieted. A few screams and hollers snowballed into an ocean-like wave of noise as fans made their way out into the concourse.

The bouncer nudged the ticket taker. "They're making the first band go on really early tonight. Pretty cruel."

The ticket taker just looked past him. "What?"

The screams were getting louder. And they weren't the screams of people having a good time. In the doorway of the Men's Room, Blond Dude held a human head—the bathroom stall guy. A new song, "Sweet Child O' Mine," came on the

PA. This Guns N' Roses band was different, but Dave liked the sound of the guitar on this single.

Black jacket slick with blood, Metallica T-shirt torn in half, The Blond Dude looked out around at the crowd like it was his personal concession stand.

Food!

He dropped the head. It rolled the head into the crowd.

For a moment, several headbangers looked like they might reach down and grab for it, which Dave thought was just a habit they'd gotten used to born from years of diving for tossed guitar picks at countless metal shows.

Blond Dude lumbered into the crowd, emitting a moaning noise that sounded like every vowel growled at once wired through a stack of Marshall amps.

Blonde Dude focused on a scrawny little guy, bit right into his neck. Fuckers screamed and yelled and ran every which way.

Andre stumbled out from the bathroom, oval hole in his neck and half his puffy hair matted down with blood. Big bruise-colored circles around his eyes.

He grabbed the closest man to him—a Morrissey-looking shorthair clad in a Depeche Mode shirt.

Morrissey reached inside the inner pocket of his jean jacket and pulled out a small spray can.

How'd he get that in? Dave thought.

Morrissey sprayed Andre in the face; Dave was sure by the purple color of the can that it was hairspray and not mace. Not like it would have made a difference because Andre was now a full on, flesh hungry zombie and simple things like hairspray, or even mace, would just be distractions.

Andre leaned in and looked like he was going in for a kiss.

When he pulled away, Morrissey's lips stretched out like rubber dental dams before they tore and ripped off.

As his kisser got mangled Dave swore he heard Andre cry-scream, *Oh, who-ah, oh.*

Chewing on a mouth full of bloody lips, Andre didn't seem satisfied and went in for a second bite.

Morrissey went down in front of Andre, grasping his mouth. Bright, pretty blood spewed from him. Behind Andre, two more undead metalheads lumbered out.

"Shit," Dave said. "I can't believe there's more."

"Sweet Child O' Mine" faded into Metallica's "Battery."

The two new zombies ran into the confused crowd—flies trapped inside a mason jar.

Dave hopped the wooden T-fence and made for the entrance. There were still people lined up, holding their tickets and gaping eagerly at the blood-drenched scene.

"Hey, man? Why're you leaving? This looks like some show!" No one understood what he was talking about. No one got it.

Outside, the mass of people waiting to get in looked at the running, blood-soaked kid and looked away. Most of them probably thought he'd gotten into a fight and got thrown out. They just stood there. Dave gave up trying to warn people. They'd figure it out, or they'd die. Wasn't his problem. His problem was getting to the New Haven train station and getting home.

He made it to the top of the huge staircase outside the Coliseum that led down to the street. People were everywhere and he smelled a cloud of pot smoke. It smelled so damn good and, shit, he could really use some. But he knew it'd only be a matter of time before the things in there got out.

Dave would have to wait to smoke up at home. Better safe than sorry, after all.

Rushing down the stairs, he tried to think of an out-of-the-way route to the train station. He wiped at his face, anxious to get as much blood off as possible: *What would the cops think about all of this?* Shit, if only there was a river or *something* around close-by . . . .

The fountain in the mall.

Yes. It was right around the corner. He could hurry there, wash up, and no one would see him. But wait. To get there, he'd have to go back up the stairs, up to the main concourse, and then back down the other side of stairs. Either that, or walk all around the Coliseum to the other side.

Fuck that. Those things were out there. Who knows where they were or could be hiding?

Three blocks to the train station, Dave told himself. *Just slip past the ticket booths and board the train. Get a ticket from the conductor after hitting the bathroom to clean up.*

Not perfect, but probably the best available course of action.Dave heard police sirens. Grateful they were behind him instead of in front of him, he hurried down the last bit of stairs, past the last big batch of metal fans and made it to the sidewalk.

Three blocks.

More sirens.

Dave heard the crowd starting to get noisy. Something was happening and he thought he'd damn near gotten out of there in the nick of time, after all. He crossed the street, jammed with cars circling the show venue and dropping people off.

Fresh blood.

He looked back up at the concourse. The doors were all closed. People were banging to get out. He spotted the bouncer holding one set of doors shut.

They'd locked them in, hadn't they? Bastards!

Dave hurried away down the first block. What else could he do?

Then, he heard the deafening roar of the crowd inside the coliseum rise. Even a block away, the roar of the crowd inside the coliseum was loud enough to hear what was happening as Maiden had just hit the stage.

Dave recognized the first notes of "The Trooper" and, for a second, was bummed he wasn't inside.

Dead or undead, that was a great fucking song.

Ahead, the train station looked deserted, devoid of even the few late night commuters he'd sometimes see.

Anyone taking a train now would be a late night commuter, and there weren't too many of those.

Dave paused at the front doors. He saw himself in the reflection and sized himself up. He didn't look drenched in blood, after all. In fact, he didn't see any on his face and his hair just looked wet. No big deal. Most of the old people in the station or on the train wouldn't look too closely at him, anyway. He was just some trashy piece of garbage to them, he knew.

The train station was deserted and Dave was relieved. He made his way to the platform, which was only a few steps beyond where he'd first entered.

Outside, he was happy to see there was a train already on the tracks. *That's right*, he thought. New Haven's one of those stops where they park the train for a few minutes between Boston and New York. Awesome.

He slipped unnoticed onto the train.

Dave made his way past a sleeping suit and tie to the car bathroom.

Instinctively, he felt his right butt cheek to make sure his wallet was still there. It was, chain and all.

Thank God.

He was going to get out of this. He had plenty cash in there, too—he never had the chance to buy the tour T-shirt.

It was all too perfect. The only other people in the train car were a couple buried deep in one of the back seats kind of going at it a little. They wouldn't be any trouble to him, he knew. The girl with the curly blond hair was on top of the guy, after all. Neither of them would give a rat's ass about him when they had each other. Great.

The strong chemical smell in the bathroom was gross and would have normally made Dave hurry up and get out as soon as he could. But he didn't care tonight. He was safe. The door had a lock on it too. So he turned on the sink and looked at himself. There was definitely a ring of blood around his face, so he started with that first.

The train jerked and he heard the high-pitched moan of its breaks unlatching. The engine rumbled to life. With a whine, he heard the doors slide closed outside.

He smiled. He'd done it. He'd gotten away. Now he only had a half-hour ride back home. *I can watch this on the news tonight,* he thought. *And I still have my concert ticket to prove I was there.*

Dave spent ten luxurious minutes in the bathroom freshening up, confident his night and his luck had taken a turn for the better.

He was wrong.

The couple met him as he opened the door.

"You guys need to get in here?" he asked.

Before he finished, he saw that the girl's eyes were sunk in and ringed with deep purple circles. Her mouth was open just a bit and Dave saw her teeth stained red from blood. The fellow she'd been on top of stared at Dave like he'd just hit his a bong twenty times. Most of his throat was missing.

Dave backed into the bathroom and grabbed for the door handle.

They weren't making out. She was fucking eating him. I'm such a dumb bastard.

Dave backed into the bathroom and grabbed for the door handle.

Too late.

The girl was on him in a flash, pushing up his chin, biting into his neck.

Dave didn't have the will to fight another war.

God, why didn't I open the door a little bit first and check?

The girl gnawed and pulled and licked. Dave could smell the minerals and the heat coming off the blood pouring out of his body. Curls of blond hair tickled him. Her forehead moved against his lips.

He kind of liked it.

If I have to go . . . .

He thought about the concert, pictured Maiden hitting the stage, the guitar notes and drums. He could almost the clouds of pot and the perfume of the girls in front of him . . . .

And then he heard Bruce Dickinson calling to him, picking him out of everyone in the crowd, just as everything faded to black.

Hope Is Just Another Four-Letter Word

John Boden

The sun rolled in its socket, a dead eye in the sky that saw nothing.

Below, the man on his dead horse carved a trail through the dry earth, dotted lines in dust and sand like ants. Like soldiers.

Over the last few days, the horse had finally stopped stinking and the quilt of flies that had swaddled them was dissipating. Troy patted the matted strings of mane that remained and the beast snorted, clots of dust and dead maggots pelting the ground below like rain. Troy groaned and patted a little harder. "Let's keep it going, Alpo," Troy urged pulling the reins a little tighter, they just cut deeper into the rotting corners of the horse's mouth so he eased up. "What the hell, it's not like I have anywhere to be in a hurry to get to." And so they slowly walked on and on and on. The sun bled from the sky, leaving a bruise.

The cars that littered the road looked like science fiction insects, metal carapaces gone faded and dusty. A green Camaro commanded Troy's attention as he stopped and hopped from his steed. He opened the driver's side door and got in. The car smelled of dried meat and sour milk. There were dark stains on the seats and windows. He leaned into the back seat and found a shoebox with some cassettes inside. He grabbed it and climbed back out into the open air, gulping gritty breaths like he'd been underwater. He gave his attention to the box in his hands. He held each tape up to his eyes and read the names. Of the ten, he kept three. Kix, Journey, and Uriah Heep. He stuffed them into the bag on his saddle and climbed back on his horse. The wind moaned through the dead cars; antennas waggled and the cracked windows shined like jewels. Troy took it all in and thought it was the most beautiful tombstone he'd ever seen. "Come on, Alpo." He jiggled the rope and the horse started walking.

Troy smiled as he remembered those *Mad Max* movies of his childhood. Just like that but for real and fewer people. The end of that thought killed his smile like a bad thought in church. He had not seen another living person in months, maybe a year. He had no way of knowing how much time had passed—the coma thing had fucked up the count. He wasn't even sure what had happened. He had been walking and had a fever. Maybe food poisoning; he'd eaten some dodgy looking food he'd found at an abandoned service station. His vision swam and blurred and the next thing he knew, he was coming to under a withered tree baptized in bird shit and painted in dust. His lips were like leather and his skin was blasted by the sun. He held up a wrist and looked at his watch. The hands were still and the date frozen. Who knew when. He smashed his watch and cried a haughty "Fuck You!" to the skies.

The sky replied by pelting him with grey rain and frogs. Almost frogs. More like squirmy little tadpole things that wriggled and nipped to get under your skin. Troy had made it to shelter in an old tin shed and watched the living rain squiggle and writhe under a cataract sky. He sat in the dim and ate fingerfuls of mud until sleep took him. The sound of the rain crawling on the tin overhead was like fingertips on a coffin lid. He slept anyway.

Three days after the rain, Troy found Alpo. The horse had been standing under the sagging overhang of a barn. Buzzards covered the ledge of the roof in a beaky black blanket and lined the rib-like timbers that remained of the structure's walls. The horse had just bowed its head and stood, chewing at a clump of crisped grass. It was already dead. Troy had approached slowly and held a hand out towards the creature. Its hide was gone as was most of the flesh beneath, mainly skeleton with a few dried organs and tatters of tissue remaining. It looked to Troy with sorrowful sockets and stepped forward, lowering its head and then slowly bringing it up into the man's palm. It snorted softly and raised its head a little. Troy patted it and the horse raised a hoof. The smell was bad but that wasn't what made Troy's eyes tear up. He had been alone so long he didn't care. He reached into the backpack he wore and pulled out a length of rope. Braided from the hair of the dead lady he found in the hospital months ago, hair and some ribbon he found in a store. He looped it around the horse's neck. "I think I'll call you Alpo." Troy smiled at his morbid sense of humor and the horse did nothing but stand. Flies buzzed and the day burned on. And Troy was no longer alone.

It was nearly a week after that Troy found the boom box. It was in a garage under a worktable. He found some batteries, still sealed in the package, still in date, and popped them in. He then went to the nearest carcass of a thrift store and plundered some more cassettes. Troy was now crossing the land to the sounds of King Diamond and Judas Priest and Whitesnake and Dio. He had filled a bag with batteries and tapes and had them tied to the saddle strap. The boom box was tied to Alpo's ribcage with an old leather belt. They kept moving and the music kept them company and the world paid them little mind. Troy paid little in return. Fuck-the-world style.

This campfire hissed and spat sparks as Troy huddled into its light to work on his jacket. A beat up leather, dirty and worn thin. He picked another incisor from the pile of teeth and pushed it through the small hole he'd made with his penknife. He did it again and again until the tooth pile was gone. He stood and laid the jacket over a large rock beside which Alpo stood. It looked awesome. The large crossbones and skull that adorned the back, painted with ash mud and blood, framed with the teeth. "Rob Halford, eat your heart out." Troy beamed, then frowned a little, "Rest in peace." Only the bottom of the skull's jaw needed studs. He'd have to wait until the found some more dead for him to get any teeth. He liked the way the gold ones danced in the firelight. It was like fireflies, he thought as he ate his can of corn.

The nights stretched like midnight taffy and coiled back to swallow like a snake. Troy found his hope withering like an unused limb. He ate what he could and rode until tired or bored, then he slept and awoke to do it again and again. Those early days found him ripe with optimism, now he was festering with guilt and grief. A world that never gave a shit about him was the thing he missed the most, oddly while this new world still didn't give a shit about him. "Life's the same except for the shoes, as the song goes." Sitting by the fire, he eats a handful of dirt, mixed with the blood from his thumb. Better than starving. Night was a chain that dragged and clanged like Jacob Marley through the quiet halls of the world.

It had to be October, maybe early November. The dark was coming sooner and it wasn't any colder. Troy wore his jacket, regardless. There seemed to really be only one speed to the weather since the world took a shit. Never unbearably hot and never too cold. Often dry. Troy leaned against the pump outside The Gas Stop and drank the flat can of root beer he'd found in the machine. Alpo grazed on the weeds that choked the side lot. Troy watched the sky; it roiled and rolled like a cancerous ocean above his head. He threw the can into a wooden crate by his feet and belched loudly. Alpo whinnied low. "I was going to say excuse me, quit nagging." He laughed at himself.

At first, Troy wanted to find a place. Somewhere that was still okay. Untouched by God's drunken fists that day. He wanted to be with people and eat food that wasn't outdated in cans or lizards roasted over a fire. He wanted to talk; he wanted to be happy. Those first weeks, hope was what got him through. Hope was the love that waited with open arms at the end of a hard hard day. Then as the empty world and longing wore him down, hope became the object of resentment and spite and he began to beat her. Then ignored her. Then she simply ceased to be, almost as though she were real.

Alpo dragged his hooves in the dirt. Making grooves. Troy untied the bags from the saddle and sat them by the edge of the concrete parking lot. He pulled a cassette from the bag and popped it into the player and hoisted himself up onto the horse. He dragged a calloused hand over exposed ribs and whispered softly, "Here we go." He looked up and Alpo replied with a soft whinny. Ahead of them was the field, and beyond its edge, the ocean. The wind cheered and Alpo took off.

Hooves pounded dry earth, creating clouds you could step on. The vocals screamed in the air. Halford.

Troy yelled "Faster!" His eyes pinned to the open sea and the field as it grew smaller. The edge of the cliff closer and closer.

They galloped and as Alpo ran out into eternity, Troy leaned in and hugged his horse. He smiled as the wind peeled back his eyes, the salt of the sea stinging them. The air caressed them as they fell. From the boom box music soared . . . .

"Die hard resolution, that is true to the end . . . ."

The sea rolled and churned.

Demon Envy: A Romance

Shawn Macomber

Ram's horns curled out from clutches of blonde and brunette hair, rising and falling, each cycle punctuated by a gunshot crack of bone striking against like, black silk nighties undulating with a dreamy slowness, as if the soiled laundry-tinged air were deep water currents—

"Girls, go easy!" cried Ollie Schwartzkowski. "I like a little buzzed, not unconscious, okay? I got standards!"

Were Ollie a man at all given to reflection, the strange fact that he could recall neither how long he'd sat slouched and agog amidst the flickering light of black and red candles inexplicably spotting his mobile home master bedroom as two mysterious women butted heads nor the circumstances of their arrival might have inspired pause, fear even. Yet aside from a brief spasm of concern over how much was paid to whom for this nutty hook-up, Ollie's main focus was moving on from peripheral voyeur before someone got it in her head to ask for more cash.

The blonde froze, balanced impossibly upon vertical toes. "Oh, standards?" she said without turning. "How wonderful for you, how unexpected for us."

Ollie massaged an amorphous patch of greying buzz cut near his temple with a palm. The brunette settled deeper into a defensive crouch, visibly relieved to no longer be a focal point, but still vigilant. She sniffed at Ollie like a wary dog, something he never saw a pretty girl do before. He involuntarily hummed a few bars from the chorus of that old Warrant power ballad . . . .

Heaven isn't too far away . . . Closer to it every day . . . .

The blonde descended into a pristine rectangle of rust-colored rug, stark against otherwise pervasive grime. Ollie wondered hopefully if steam cleaning might be part of the kink until he realized the demoness stood where his mattress had always lain. Eyes now unglued from the main event, new details emerged from the landscape: Disgorged springs and stuffing strewn about the room, mottled with shards of Pop's sole bequeathal to Ollie, an old solid oak dresser. Threadbare wifebeaters, torn stonewashed jeans, dilapidated boxers—it looked as if a rural Goodwill store had been truck-bombed.

"Molting," the blonde said, jerking a sideways, eye rolling nod at her partner.

The brunette accepted the recognition as an invitation to sidle up and stroke her horn against the other's spiraling bone. The blonde's spinning roundhouse butt passed Ollie in a merciless blur, sending the brunette crashing into a shadowed pile of bedchamber rubble. The alpha gave a few nonexistent wrinkles in her nightie a nonchalant, dainty smoothing then, as if at last properly prepared, beckoned Ollie with a suggestive smile.

No matter what your friends might say . . . I know we're gonna find a way . . . .

Despite the violence, Ollie did not hesitate. Not when a

disparaging snort wafted out anonymously from a darkened corner or the walls bled outlines of red, circled stars, or even as the blonde's eyes went inkwell black and, folding her arms, she dismissed gravity like a schoolgirl defying a nerveless stepfather.

It took welts, aglow like embers, swelling up in the shape of an oval-topped "T" on the blonde's chest to slow Ollie's automaton march.

"Problem, Ollie?" she asked, following his gaze, tracing the scalded lines and curves.

"You girls, like, feminists or something?"

"Do we look like feminists to you?"

Ollie shrugged. In truth he didn't know. Feminists were like jersey devils in his family, mythical monsters one heard fearsome tell of but never actually saw.

"Lesbians?"

"That," she said, tapping his nose twice with a thick, opaque fingernail, "is a part-time orientation tonight."

Ollie was still mentally neutering the bull of apprehension as the shadows descended.

The brunette floated above him, arms raised like Daniel-san doing the crane kick at the end of *The Karate Kid*, forked tongue too perfectly matching her hiss, wrong rack cocked toward him.

Ollie did not feel the blow, only fell into a buzzy, gentle swoon. A coven cackled nearby. Ollie heard a gurgling, hoped it wasn't a sucking chest wound . . . .

He opened his eyes. His bent legs hung in the air before him. A capsized Natural Light dribbled its contents onto the rug. The Lay-Z-Boy had tipped over backwards. Television. *The View*. A dream. And some major piece of shit pounding away at the door.

"Fucking okay already," Ollie shouted, rocking his body

out of the recliner. He pulled his track pants up from around his knees—not that unusual for the morning after a drinking night, actually—and stumbled toward the unknown intruder. Better be good. Ollie didn't volunteer for tannery furlough to play early bird for no worm.

"Hey there, Oliphant."

Bianca Day bounced lightly on the bowing plank of Ollie's makeshift bucket and board doorstep. She wore an oversized men's sport jacket festooned with patches of mallpunk band logos and *Nightmare Before Christmas* characters, and a wide smile with a side of unsubtle eye batting. A pewter ankh hung from her glorified dog collar, the symbol from the blonde's chest—wet dream become nightmare. Silently, Ollie started to close the door.

"No, please, wait!"

Ollie paused, feigning interest in a couple robins tap dancing amongst the pine needles atop a rusting heating oil tank. Bianca glanced back, sighed. The birds, unused to the attention, froze. Park denizens ate all manner of nontraditional cuisine, and the wildlife instinctively sensed it.

"Alright, look, Ollie, I didn't mean for everyone to make jokes."

Ollie snorted. Worst of it was, inviting Bianca over made Ollie feel like the Mother Teresa of Sherwood Glen—a saint rejecting superficiality with an act of sexual charity. Always sitting on the porch of her ma's trailer next door, alone, boombox blasting songs about death by the transvestite du jour, stupid goddamned dog collar choking unflattering neck heft up into those cadaver pale jowls that glowed behind a string curtain of dye-fried black hair. Add bruise-purple eye shadow that evaded any respectable aesthetic boundaries and the flat, upturned nose—you had a wigged bulldog with a matching pair of shiners and shit taste in music. And you didn't expect a wigged bulldog with a matching pair of shiners and shit taste in music to respond to a little masculine attention by blabbing to the chain smokers down at the park mail hut about chicken pot pie foreplay and come-ons during commercial breaks of *Billy Madison*.

So Ollie didn't exactly roll out the red carpet for Her Majesty. Now she had to go steady with her doppelganger and make him the laughingstock of every park MILF he'd been creeping on to boot? That was the sort of bullshit that made heaven seem very fucking far away.

"You know these park assholes," Bianca said, craning her neck to resettle a plot on Ollie's field of vision. "They exaggerate everything. I didn't say nothing that bad, I swear."

"Sure. Whatever. That all?"

Ollie wanted to sound callous, aloof, but he went from scanning the yard for evidence of a prank to goggling Bianca's overstressed fishnets and casually sucking his gut in.

"No, I brought a peace offering."

Bianca pulled a small box—black and fuzzy like Ollie's ma's old velour tunic—from a Hello Kitty messenger bag.

"Totally fancy, right?" Bianca cooed. Ollie rattled the box next to his ear and caught Bianca trying to mask a grimace. So he shook it again, a little harder. "Promise to use it this morning, and I'll come over tonight to make sure you're satisfied. Deal?"

Ollie was way too eager to refurbish his park reputation to snub this Jezebel's offer, whatever her game. Not to mention the begging, he liked.

"Yeah, okay, maybe.

The thought of relegating Bianca's package unopened to the pile of detritus gradually overtaking Ollie's kitchen nook was seriously tempting. Let it serve as a single stratum on Mount Drunken Infomercial amongst the layers of softcore DVDs, BMG CDs, color-coded past due notices, telephone bill itemization pages mirroring the alt-weekly phone sex ads, half-assembled D-list celebrity endorsed exercise gear, and, out on Irony Ridge, personal finance audiobooks.

Still, the embossing piqued his interest.

MONSTER CLUB

"Let Your Member Be A Member"

A flick of a brass latch released a spring-loaded hinge. The top rose revealing a brown Tootsie Roll-sized winged gargoyle encircled by red silk ruffle, painstakingly detailed. Ollie plucked the pill from its ornate chamber and tweezed a tiny scroll from diminutive talons.

ENTICE. ENKINDLE. ENGORGE. ENLIVEN.

Lilitu's Promise: Total Penile Metamorphosis

(Swallow Whole)

Ollie chuckled ruefully. He gave up Ponce de Leon-ing for this particular elusive manspring-wellspring long ago after investing thousands without registering so much as a quarter-inch return on that damned indifferent, frigid plastic ruler. The ManJack, a hundred dollar hermetically sealed electric penis pump, served as sad apotheosis to that quixotic quest on a birthday spent alone watching *Tango and Cash* and, yes, feasting on chicken pot pie.

Well, hopefully Bianca would be hungry tonight. She'd be eating the wholesale on this one. Door-to-door scam . . . girl had some gall, but Ollie wasn't choosing between cable and heat to secure her good graces. There'd probably be some *oohs* and *ahhs* at a supposed bulge, then the hard sell: *Park husbands will be chaining their wives to radiators! Three easy installments! Closé, personal friend discount!*

The small print set Ollie's head pounding. Time to talk to Bronson. Grab bag John Doe doses were cheaper, sure, but hangovers and hot lesbian demon hallucinations only kicking your ass left plenty to be desired from one's recreational drugs. Ollie sank into the chair, fading fast, until a kvetching whine from the foggy distance reeled him back from the clutches of stalking oblivion.

"This schmuck in Monster Club?" Joy Behar said. "Looks like a big sis to me."

"You kidding?" Whoopi retorted. "Ollie is mah man, aren't you Ollie?"

Ollie raised an eyelid half-mast. Whoopi Goldberg—she of the totally underrated *Jumpin' Jack Flash*, heart and soul of *Ghost*—pressed her nose to the television screen peeping out as if through a window.

"That bloated battle-ax is not gonna win this burrito bet. 'Cause you gonna swallow, right, Ol? *Hah ha*! Oh, yeah . . . he gonna swallow, alright."

As susceptible to her charms as those stuffy *Sister Act* choir nuns, Ollie nudged the pill into his mouth. He toyed with the idea of retrieving a brew to wash it down, but the gargoyle spelunked along his parched tongue and down his throat, almost, it seemed, of its own volition.

That's mah man, Ollie. Mah man.

Imagine tending for thirty-one years a garden that never produced anything save puny string beans and one morning finding it teeming with luscious baby squash. Imagine yourself a meek tadpole, resigned to froggy future when a telegraph arrives—*Maternity ward mix-up! Your real parents are Amazonian anacondas.* Imagine an instantaneous, unexpected, utter end to an inadequacy previously thought incurable. Imagine *revenge.*

Three hours after swallowing the gargoyle, Ollie awoke so crackly and cranked he half expected to find a Red Bull IV plugged into his arm. He bounded toward the bathroom humming the *Dukes of Hazard* theme. The tune slowed to a dirge as a strange new density filled his palm. He stared into the eyes of his Stone Cold Steve Austin poster as he gave one last tentative, exploratory squeeze, and . . . no shit.

Cease seeking glory, and it arrives unbidden!

Ollie tugged and twisted his new supercharged manhood with the mien of a puppeteer breaking in a new marionette. He swung it like a grandfather clock pendulum, wound it like a coiled snake, stretched it like breadstick dough. When he finally took his piss, a tar black thimbleful of thick goo, blowtorch hot, dribbled out—an eminently endurable side effect, all things considered.

Ollie called Bronson, demanded product, pronto. No cash. No problem.

Bronson would be begging Ollie for a fix soon enough. Ollie spent the brief interlude fantasizing about launching a Lilitu's Promise franchise ("I'm not only Monster Club's president, I'm also a client"), a cadre of young women like Bianca—hotter even!—earning livelihoods at his filthy rich pleasure.

Bronson arrived looking like a shell-shocked Western front

soldier circa-1918, if Doughboys' uniforms consisted of athletic shorts, an I'd Fuck Me T-shirt, and an avant-garde bedhead helmet. The dealer nodded toward Ollie's bedroom, which appeared to be barfing its half-digested contents into the hallway. He widened bloodshot eyes rather than vocalize the question.

"Whatever you were pushing last night must make Ollie go cuckoo!" Ollie said, chuckling nervously through a stinging nettle of adrenaline.

"Nah, bro, you putting that on me—I had your shit, but you zombie-walked out of the bar. With Bianca. Who, not for nothing, you supposedly hate. So I sold it to Jimmy. If Jimmy fuck up yo bedroom, that ain't got shit to do with me."

As Ollie struggled to stitch a response from scraps of befuddlement and foreboding, a low growling voice from below preempted him.

Your mother is a reincarnated Moabite whore!

"This some ventriloquist shit, Ol? Very funny."

She committed unspeakable acts of sexual perversity in my name, Baal-Peor—

"Fuck you say 'bout my mother?"

— she will spend eternity fellating Marduk, gargling lava cum in a bathroom stall of resurrected Babylon.

Ollie stiffened. He worked to convince himself he felt neither the serpentine stirring against his leg nor an exhalation against his thigh. Ollie sprinted past Bronson to the bathroom, kicked the door closed, and gingerly tugged the elastic waistband from beneath a flabby gut overhang. A few reassuring seconds of stillness, and then Ollie's burgeoning penis wobbled up. The meatus slit spoke:

Lord Baal demands sustenance.

The door creaked. Bronson leaned in.

"Yo, Ol, shake it more than twice, you're playing with yourself."

Polish the purple helmet of my petite warrior, fefe boy!

"Look, bad trip or not, you want your ass beat, Ol, it can be arranged! I will do that for you fo sho. Just go ahead and say one more thing about my . . . . "

Ollie spun, wheezing, beseeching hands extended to his dealer. The liberated penis bobbed and darted, gleaming rows of new serrated teeth snapping.

Bite me off this philistine!

Bronson dove out a hallway window. It was closer than the door. He took the aluminum frame, part of the wall, and several deep gashes with him. At the entrance to Sherwood Glen he fell hysterical and bloodied into arms of a gaggle of Jehovah Witnesses plotting the day's proselytizing.

Rarely thereafter did Bronson ever stray far from the Kingdom Hall.

Lord Baal lay curled in Ollie's lap snoring, thanks to an Ambien snuck into a glob of raw hamburger. Ollie emptied the fuzzy box. No phone number, no web address. He swiveled, peered out the window. Bianca's trailer sat dark and silent. What to do? The free clinic downtown was out—this was Blue Cross shit at least. Recognizing he needed a miracle, Ollie strained to retrieve his tattered Yellow Pages from the just-within-reach end table, flipped to Churches, Etc., and dialed the number on the first full-page ad.

"Our Lady of Perpetual Exasperation's 24-hour absolution line, Father McMurty speaking."

"Yes, I'm battling a demonic—"

"One absolution is forty dollars or three for a hundred."

"Just one."

"Got fewer than two sins left in you?"

"Hard times, father."

"Harder in Hell, I'll wager. Still, as you wish."

Ollie recited his Visa number, crossed his fingers waiting for authorization—itself a minor miracle.

"Alrighty, Christ standeth here invisibly, be not ashamed and conceal thou nothing from me. In other words, what's up?"

"Father, this'll sound crazy, but—"

"I cannot hear a thing you're saying."

"Sorry, I'm trying not to wake . . . him."

"Him who?"

"Baal-Peor, I think."

"Baal-Peor?"

Be not ashamed, conceal nothing . . . .

"The . . . demon in my pants."

"Uh huh. Father Landry!"

An expert on this kind of phantasm, perhaps?

"Hewow. Is this the naughty young man with the lustful little tallywhacker that needs smiting?"

Or not.

"Father, no, this is a for real possession—"

"Trust a former randy young man who knows what it takes to, hmm, rub out certain demons. Let me reauthorize for the Special Services surcharge . . . . "

"Please, father, listen—"

"Sure, sure, you've some very filthy things to confess, no doubt and . . . oh. Oh dear, insufficient funds. Have another credit card?"

"Um, no."

"Tried a porno? In the name of the Father, Son and the Holy—"

The line went dead before the priest gave up the ghost.

Forsaken, Ollie set about putting his affairs in order. Note for Ma. Bag up Mount Drunken Infomercial Order. Last meal. (Salisbury steak TV dinner?) Feed Siamese fighting fish. Leap into Old Reston Quarry—short drive, long fall, deep water, jagged rocks . . . .

For now, why jostle sleeping Baal before absolutely necessary? Ollie grabbed the remote to erase the softcore off his DVR spank bank. Maybe set it to record a few Discovery Channel shows. A little refinement red herring so his family wouldn't feel like deputized failure archeologists excavating the trailer after his body bloated and floated.

The Skinimax free trial treated me well, Ollie mused wistfully as he scrolled down the recorded programs list. Life is funny. One day you're watching *Police Interrogators: Wildest Suspect Beatdowns*, the next a penile phantasm forces you to commit suicide, never to enjoy the dramatic reenactments of, say, *Monster Car Wrecks: I Swerved to Miss Bigfoot* or . . . .

"The fuck?" Ollie said to himself, sounding out the words of the next show: "*Countdown to Cat-ah-clysm With Aosoth?*"

Ollie clicked play. An eight-armed, no-handed woman with a bad perm and a glistening black thorax paced a soundstage. The blonde horned she-beast from his dream sat on a couch watching the spider lady work the studio audience while the brunette obliterated a coffee table emblazoned with The View logo just offstage. (Still molting, apparently.) Thick, meaty masks of Whoopi and Joy hung impaled on sticks, dripping large dollops of fat.

"Alright, let's take some calls," Aosoth said in a snappy torrent unhindered by her foot-long underbite. She pressed an earpiece with one of her churning nubs, yellow eyes shining, multiple irises swirling. "Wow, the legendary Pazuzu is on the line! Care to give us the bad word on this momentous night, Pazu-baby?"

"Yes, certainly my dear Aosoth. What your viewers must realize is . . . *THE POWER OF CHRIST COMPELS YOOOUUUU! THE POOOOOWER . . . .* "

"Gaaahaarrr," roared Aosoth. Her thorax snapped open like a clamshell, tentacles swarming out from the deep black cavity. A small white cyclone swirled in the center. In his medicated slumber, Baal murmured depraved motifs in Latin. Aosoth regained her composure, picking her perm with two nubs while another pair wrestled the thorax closed.

"That wasn't very ladylike," she said to cheers. "Nice try, Father Karras. Hope you're enjoying Sixth Circle Geriatric Center diaper duty. Anywho, next caller. Abezethibou? Ya hear me?"

"Yes, Aosoth, your voice is sweet as boiling oil upon a peasant's head."

"Abeze-y, you gonna make me blush, boy. Flattery will get you almost everywhere. Now what's on your mind?"

"Okay, so, the prophecy is fulfilled, crybaby Christ is probably having a conniption—I'm sitting here on an Israelite bone throne in my bathrobe wondering if a certain venomous harlot will shed a little exoskeleton to commemorate the event?"

Aosoth placed several nubs on her hips, and shook her

head slowly, as the room erupted into catcalls and whoops.

"This bod? Demon, please! You'll have to put a whole goddamn lot of hours in at the gym before that is a possibility, playa . . . . "

A number flittered across the screen: 1-666-SIN-2WIN. Dazed, without a plan, Ollie dialed. A producer answered, second ring.

"Name?"

"Steven Seagal."

Marked for Death had been on Spike two nights ago.

"The Steven Seagal?"

"Uh, yep. Under siege and out for justice."

"Turn your television volume down. Hold for Aosoth."

Ollie complied. An echoing loop of tortured screams blared in his ear. Damnation's Muzak. Onscreen, Aosoth mouthed a few words in close-up. Dissolve to a grainy green night vision shot. Ollie floats naked in midair. The prodding blonde she-beast playing natural scientist to his tranquilized walrus couldn't quite supersede Ollie's blushing dread at his shockingly tire-like televised spare tire, but the image of the brunette dragging Bianca over, pricking her finger, and guiding it to smear a bloody inverted cross slightly above Ollie's groin sure did. Ollie slid a hand down. Shaved, itchy. Still, Ollie felt a strange pang of excitement—he was on television!

Fade out. Fade in.

Ollie, still levitating, is crammed into a she-beast nightie, spinning above pizza boxes and Natural Light empties while the blonde and Bianca take giggly, drunken turns snaring Ollie's head in pairs of his own dirty underwear. The brunette takes crashing leaps at Pop's dresser . . . .

"Steve-o!" Aosoth boomed—earth/Hell time delay? "An honor! *Under Siege 2: Dark Territory* is our go-to torture device for Victorians, uppity professorial types, art house cinema snobs! Tell me, is it as painful for you to admit you were in that movie as it is for us to watch it?"

"I give all credit for its badness," Ollie quipped with what wry wisecracking toughness he could muster, "to Katherine Heigl."

The crowd roared its approval. Seagal, so self-deprecating, so down to earth!

"Okay, before I start badgering you for behind the scenes scuttlebutt, why ya callin' me instead of practicing Zen skull-crackin' or texting Dana White selfies or sumpthin'?"

"Right, well, I'm just curious, why Ollie? Seems like a cool guy."

"Seriously? Seagal! You're a worse judge of dudes than scripts! J/K, man! Uh, we set our bead on Ollie after his neighbor told this hilarious story to a poltergeist on Ouija board duty about a chicken pot pie . . . . "

Fuck-all, is it too much to ask people keep their gossiping to the realm of the living!?

". . . and, actually, we've been seeking a suitable reanimation vessel for a loooong time. Conscience, fear of damnation, the upstairs do-gooder gang's meddling—it ain't easy down here for a spirit pimp!"

An Aosoth staffer with a gaggle of garter snakes for hair threw her hands up to raise the imaginary roof. "Heeeyyyy, ho-ohhh!" the audience chanted. Aosoth laughed, swayed her own arms briefly.

"It's been an exciting time. Order came down from Old Splitfoot, 'Think outside the box,' so we all read *Who Moved*

My Cheese?, Jack Welch's autobiography, *The Secret*—basically thought positively about negative outcomes, brainstormed, and not long ago finally had a breakthrough. Steve, where does the purest concentration of lust, gluttony, greed, pride, wrath, and envy reside in the human body do you think?"

"The heart?"

"Nope."

"The mind?"

"Try lower, friend. Hint, it's the where baby batter gathers!"

"Um . . ."

"Yes, the male sex organ is an *amazing* recruitment tool," the blonde she-beast interjected, exhaling a mushroom cloud cigarette smoke plume. "Tell a scorned woman, 'You know what Christianity calls those glandular secretions making your man want to spread his seed around your circle of friends? Intelligent Design!' Sister girlfren' is desecrating holy grounds before you can say, 'Boo!'"

"Penis possession is also strategic," Aosoth said. "Men celebrate abnormal growth down there. And archangels are such homophobes. They're not going anywhere near a dick—not for Jesus, Mohammed, Buddha or the Jolly Green Giant."

"And Bianca?"

"Easiest. Recruit. Ever. We just promised to enslave the *Twilight* chick to her. Next thing you know she's conjuring succubus and becoming Lord Baal's corporeal emissary."

"You can deliver *Twilight* souls?"

"Nah, we're just good fibbers." Aosoth drew a nub saucily to her lips. "Hadn't you heard?" Hoots, cheers. "Girl's gonna learn the mosh pit at a Marilyn Manson concert's got nothing on us, though, when we betray her live, Friday night, eight p.m.

Tune in! More Stevie Seagal after this break."

The deranged Muzak returned. Ollie placed the receiver against his chest. From the closet came a stifled whimper. He placed it immediately: *Bianca Day*.

"Why?" he shouted at the closed door.

"I was curious!"

"About girls? Or the devil?"

"Both!"

Bianca flung the door open, kicking her way from a morass of mud-crusted shitkickers and fat-slicked tannery aprons.

"Great. Well, just in case you're still curious, demon elbows in your nutsack smarts like a motherfucker."

"Not digging the 'tude, Ol. Think I'd better just deal directly with Lord Baal."

Bianca's irises fluttered, contorted into narrower slits. Black nail polish flaked as yellowed claws replaced fingertips. Bone plates creaked, horns corkscrewed outward. "I got half my pay upfront," Bianca said, rising up on her toes, a rabid ballerina, en avant, stalking Ollie backward.

At the kitchen threshold Bianca charged, but wound up surfing past Ollie in slapstick pantomime atop a cascade of *Girls Gone Wild* DVDs—*the fine print in their subscription policy is so misleading*, Ollie thought—yet she nevertheless managed a glancing blow that set him jittering like a Charismatic on Good Friday straight into Mount Drunken Infomercial Order, setting off an upending quake.

Ollie landed amongst the rubble. Bianca swooped in, straddled him, hissing and chomping. Plastic packaging and torn cardboard cut into Ollie's back. He struggled to restrain her with one hand on her throat while the other pawed debris frantically for a weapon, dreading the telltale *snap* of a forearm compound fracture.

Ollie's fingertips grazed a rubber-padded handle. He smiled. On the sole occasion he used the Ab Roller Ollie had pulled a groin muscle, so he well understood the pain it could inflict. Ollie pressed the wheel against Bianca's sternum, rolled her upright until the rubber tread rested under her chin, and then hopped up into a crouch. His isolated abdominals burned as he drove Bianca back into a tangled rat's nest of jumbo exercise bands, giant Chinese finger traps, in essence, which mollusked quickly onto her feet.

Bianca went down. Ollie followed, taken off guard by the strength of her thrusting hips beneath him. Her claws stung his chest and neck. He continued bludgeoning, but the plastic Ab Roller handles pinged impotent against matured horns. Cold fear gripped Ollie. Bianca would soon overpower him. He surveyed the room for possible escape routes, and caught glimpse of his Excalibur a few inches above her head.

ManJack!

Bianca betrayed no recognition of the hermetically sealed discount electric penis pump yet the sinister joy written across Ollie's face clearly spooked her. As he fiddled with the machine's vast array of buttons she shredded her way into the crotch of his track pants and stroked ferociously.

"Arise Dark One!"

The beast trembled to life. Ollie plunged the whirring ManJack over Bianca's snarling yap. Nothing save an annoyed gurgle came forth. A twinkle replaced the panic in Bianca's eyes. Close the circuit. Ollie seized Bianca's nostrils. Her cheeks cratered, eyeballs jiggled like Jell-o, and a buxom, deep-red, four-inch she-demon rode into the tube astride Bianca's suctioned tongue.

Roll with it or you'll go insane.

Ollie, careful not to break the seal, joggled the ManJack until the monster lost grip of Bianca's tongue stud. It smacked against the dome, scraping at Crisco-like remnants. A string of high-register obscenities followed. Bianca collapsed into wide-mouthed, unconscious palpitations, an epileptic fish out of water.

Ollie walked the ManJack to the kitchen sink and clicked it off. The demon gripped the lip of the drain. "It's too late, you're gonna pass Armageddon like a kidney stone," she squeaked.

Ollie twisted the tap on and let the garbage disposal do the holiest work of its previously undignified career, the sermon a geyser of red pulp and cheeping cries of, "What a world, what a world, what a world . . . . "

A one-man three-legged race team, Ollie lurched across the street toward Lowell Hennessy's aluminum shed. Baal chawed thigh. Warm blood flowed. No time for a quarry dive. Ollie broke the cheap padlock easily. The hedge clipper blades gleamed in a corner behind the one-tenth acre riding lawnmower.

"Pa say you could?"

Before Ollie could spit out a one-word fib the last vestiges of his tighty-whitey prison yielded to the flesh battering ram. Nine-year-old Bobby Hennessy tore off, yelling. Ollie heard the screen door slam and hoped Lowell, a hardass's hardass, wasn't home. Either way—goodbye private battle, hello public spectacle. Ollie plopped down onto the Hennessy's preternaturally green lawn. The metamorphosis was well underway. Petite Tyrannosaurus Rex arms sprouted from his shaft, clutching at the ground, seeking traction. Pubic hair unfurled in wide razor wire arcs. Baal's hideous face writhed behind the flesh veil, horny black skull crowning from the meatus slit. Sunlight danced upon a veiny sail of stretched scrotum skin.

Baal rose, feinted left, parried right, slipped the jab, and rang Ollie's bell, blinding him with overripe jock cheese. Ollie sobbed and flailed wildly at his toddler-sized cock.

"What's going on?" the meth lab proprietor shouted from his window.

"Pot pie Ollie is wrestling a pig!"

"No, that's the Sullivan's husky retard," another corrected. "Running around naked. Again."

Through a dirty blur Ollie saw Bianca sauntering through the gathering gape-mouthed scrum, lips red and voluptuous from the ManJack.

"My Lord, let me free you," she said.

At her voice, Baal erected. Bianca embraced the demon as he taunted Ollie:

See what a real man can do with this tool?

The parasitic blood transfusion had Ollie surrendering to the comforting blackness, resigned to being torn apart from the inside.

And then came Baal's scream.

Treason!

Invigorating blood rushed into Ollie's tingling head. Bianca had lashed her dog collar just under the amniotic sac of Baal's mushroom head, and grasped the ankh, dragging the demon down. The warping pewter charm began to give. Bianca wrapped a fist in an Allman Brothers Band-worthy length of pubic hair.

"No, Bianca, run, get to a church, any church . . . well, not

Our Lady of Perpetual Exasperation unless you absolutely have no other choice, but, yeah, other than that, basically any other church!"

"You saved my soul with that mattress pump. I won't abandon you."

"Right . . . *mattress pump!*"

Ollie felt a surge of energy from some unknown source—*love?*—and straining every video game atrophied arm and leg muscle he possessed hoisted his torso off the ground before the subject of the ManJack's purpose could be revisited. Slowly he crabwalked toward the back of the shed, Bianca wrestling Baal every step of the way.

Ollie was tantalizingly close to the hedge clippers when he felt Baal and Bianca snag on the riding lawnmower. He dropped down flat on his back and stretched an arm out. His fingers grazed the rounded wooden nub of the hedge clippers, but a grip proved elusive. Ollie placed a foot on the tire of the lawnmower and pressed hard. He felt some of the stress lines in his groin break out into open wounds. He continued to push and tear, gaining centimeters, working toward an inch.

At last he curled his fingers around the handles, sat up, pulled the handles apart and brought the well-oiled open blades down, flush with his crotch. He let a little halting sob go, then clapped the handles home. His crotch erupted, a Roman candle ejaculation of sparks and the pungent sulfur.

The light show sputtered out. A single charred leg jutted from the taco night saucepan-like mess between Ollie's legs.

"We came, we saw . . . we kicked its ass," the meth lab guy said, taking a drag on his cigarette. Bianca shot him a withering look. "Uh, *Ghostbusters*?" Nothing. "Venkman?" Annoyance.

"C'mon, everyone loves Venkman!"

Ollie slowly raised a trembling thumbs up.

"See, that's what I'm talking about!" Meth said.

Bianca shrugged her shoulders then, eyes widening in horror, pointed past them.

In the dissipating smoke Baal hopped on his remaining leg, shuffling off the baggy flesh Ollie had lovingly, if too frequently, caressed, flapping blood, pus and smegma off his wings. Baal surveyed the shocked faces with satisfaction, then began his harangue beneath a blackening sky.

The First Shepherd's dictatorship falls! Sheep, embrace freedom! Worship idols! Covetousness is the new black! Shop on Sundays! Fornicate in the str—

Two loud, earthshaking booms silenced Baal. Lowell Hennessy marched through the crowd toting a shotgun, Kiss the Cook apron over his rural route carrier uniform. Sweat set his high-and-tight haircut gleaming. Baal squirmed on the ground, a grapefruit-sized hole in either wing.

"I already go to Wal-Mart on Sundays after church," Lowell said, "and I truck no fornicating on my lawn." He turned. "This is a barbeque," Lowell declared, waving conspiratorially toward approaching police sirens. "End of story." Lowell lifted Baal aloft by his single leg, "And this here is . . . . "

"A monster that crawled out of Pot pie Ollie's peter," Bobby Hennessy answered.

"Don't be a damn fool, son. It's a . . . you know, a wild turkey."

The sins of the father shall—

Lowell flicked a wrist strengthened by two decades of mail sorting. The demon's head cracked against the deck post.

Incredulous, Bobby opened his mouth. Lowell raised a debate-ending palm.

"Take them burgers off the grill, boy."

Bobby ran off. Lowell gave the dazed Baal a vicious shake.

"Turkey!"

Everyone nodded, unsure of whom to fear more.

"You're all invited to stay. I suggest you do, on account of Mrs. Hennessy's rarely indulged love of company and her extraordinary patience with this here unplanned lawn party."

As the procession filed toward the backyard, Ollie crab-crawled toward his trailer.

"Not so fast Mister No Job Dilly Dally." Lowell untied his apron, tossed it over Ollie's midsection like a tablecloth. "You know, I had a cock demon once, too. Fixed it with some tweezers and a little rum, all without parading bare-assed across a God-fearing neighbor's well-kept lawn. Imagine that."

Ollie nodded.

"Stick around till the bird's cooked, son. And grow the fuck up."

Wild turkeys don't typically shriek in Aramaic for two hours while they barbeque, or require three men to hold a grill hood down to keep them in. The charade nevertheless proceeded unmolested. A sheriff's deputy showed up, spent more time looking suspicious than not, but ultimately gave Ollie a written warning for illegal fireworks and fucked off. On the Hennessy's back deck a couple neighbors shot Ollie apologetic looks as they partook of the gamey meat. Bianca brought him a plate of potato salad, which he pushed around with a fork until Lowell signaled he could leave. "Sherwood Glen takes out its own garbage," the buzzed patriarch called after them, with a triumphant shake of a fist. Bobby escorted the pair to the lawn's edge, I'm-not-buying-this-grown-up-bullshit stink eye the whole way.

The cookout continued into the night. Something about the meal brought out a mild licentiousness in the crowd. Mrs. Hennessy even downed a light beer. It was such a success Sherwood Glen inaugurated an annual Wild Turkey Day. Without any actual wild turkeys, however, the festival devolved into an unofficial Whiskey & Domestic Abuse Day and was soon discontinued.

One year and a gender reassignment surgery later, Olive Schwartzkowski and Bianca Day purchased a doublewide in Forest Glade on the other side of town. Olive never spoke of sacrificing her only begotten meat hammer so that the world should not perish into darkness or the subsequent romance that blossomed from betrayal during rehabilitation from the wounds suffered in the battle. But whenever *Billy Madison* showed up on basic cable Bianca microwaved a chicken pot pie, stroked Olive's cheek, and praised the force of destiny.

Author Biographies and Story Notes

On a cold winter's day in 1970, **John Boden** was born. The years since have been filled with Star Wars action figures, cartoons, books, family, life, and love. He currently resides in Pennsylvania, between the capitol and Three Mile Island. A bakery worker by day, his evenings are spent with his beautiful wife and sons, and working with Shock Totem Publications. He writes when he can and reads all the time, working sleep in where convenient.

His work has appeared in *52 Stitches, Metazen, Black Ink Horror 7, Weirdyear, Necon E-Books, Shock Totem, Blight Digest, Splatterpunk,* the John Skipp-edited *Psychos, Once Upon An Apocalypse,* and *Robbed Of Sleep.* His "not-really-for-children-even-though-it-looks-like-it" book, *Dominoes,* is a thing that's out there.

He smells a bit but he has a heart of gold.

Hope Is Just Another Four-Letter Word: I was invited to submit to this anthology, and was thrilled and flattered. Being a fan of metal as well as a fan of the editors, I figured I needed to come up with something nifty. I wanted to write a weird western thing. Well, maybe a post-apocalyptic thing about a metalhead youth facing a lonely world. But I wanted it to have a horse in it, a dead horse. And a badass leather jacket. And some metal. As is usually the case, what I wanted and what I churned out were not the same. I seem to always bring the sadness in my stories. I did manage to shoehorn in all those elements I wanted, though. I want to expand this one day.

Andrew Bonazelli was the managing editor of *Decibel Magazine* from 2005 until 2016 and is the author of a bunch of crap you can find on Amazon or Towering Achievements. The short film adaptation of "Real Mature" features Adrienne Barbeau and music from SubRosa.

Real Mature, from which this excerpt comes, will be adapted into a short film by Los Angeles-based company, Fright-O-Verse, in 2015.

Jesse Bullington has been listening to metal since forever, pretty much, especially when writing. It comes through in his work, with synopses of his three award-nominated novels reading like liner notes: In *The Sad Tale of the Brothers Grossbart*, big-bearded graverobbers pillage their way across medieval Europe and North Africa, encountering madmen, monsters, and witches. In *The Enterprise of Death*, an apprentice necromancer has adventures both carnal and macabre in her quest to recover a forbidden grimoire. *The Folly of the World* features a band of criminals exploring a flooded graveyard and stirring up a horror from the depths; after that, things get weird. He's also the editor of the critically acclaimed anthology *Letters to Lovecraft* and the co-editor (with Molly Tanzer) of the forthcoming *Swords v. Cthulhu*. He's got a few more schemes going, which you can investigate online at www.jessebullington.com and all the usual places.

October Wedding is a rare example of my juvenilia, written back when all I did was listen to metal, smoke cloves, drink shitty coffee, and scribble in notebooks. I say it's rare because most of what I produced in those early days will never see the light of day, or night for that matter, because it's beyond terrible. This story, though, I always retained a certain fondness for, and when I heard about this project I realized it would be a perfect fit. That's because while the vast majority of my work can't be traced back to a single band, this piece is essentially Cradle of Filth fanfiction. I know the band has legions of haters, but I don't give a fuuuuuuck; *Cruelty and the Beast* came out when I was in high school, and I've been hooked ever since. I wrote this story not long after seeing them in concert for the first time, and drawing inspiration from their decadent sound and rich lyrics, I committed myself to actually knuckling down and producing something every bit as darkly opulent as their music. How unexpected and exciting, then, that years later I'm able to share it with my fellow metalheads, and for such a great cause.

Tim Deal is a writer, editor, adjunct professor, and a Bram Stoker Award nominee. His work has appeared in a number of published anthologies, magazines, newspapers, and websites. He is also one of the Four Horsemen, the hosts of the annual Anthology Conference (AnthoCon). He holds an MFA in writing and runs Shroud Publishing LLC.

1988 Behind the 9:30 Club was based on a real life experience I had back in the 80s when I was at the 9:30 for a Fleshtones show. I was on a weekend pass from Fort Bragg, NC, and I had met a girl at the club that seemed totally out of place.

Sean Frasier is a writer, music journalist, and illustrator from a remote farm in upstate New York. As a screenwriter his work has been a finalist in the Nicholl Fellowship competition as well as Scriptapalooza, Screamfest, Shriekfest, and Slamdance. His feature-length horror/comedy *Hipster Massacre* is currently being produced in the UK, set for a 2016 release. Sean is a staff writer for *Decibel Magazine* and *About Heavy Metal.* His writing also appears monthly in the Los Angeles-based art zine *Kung Fu Breakfast.* He has various scars from injuries suffered during sets by Eyehategod, Opeth, and Birdflesh. He currently lives in Brooklyn, NY.

Forest of Anguish is the first zombie story I ever wrote, and it had been collecting dust on my hard drive as a concept for a future short film— an idea made infinitely more expensive by including a skinless dog as a key character. When I was invited to participate in *The Healing Monsters* I had just interviewed the fantastic Swedish band Anguish about their album, *Mountain* for *Decibel Magazine.* Through our correspondence their vocalist, David, told me about a potentially haunted cabin they used for their promo shoot. I was inspired to dig up the skeleton of my old short story, turned the protagonist into a stoner metal drummer, and couldn't help but include a few nods to the band along the way.

Larissa Glasser is an academic librarian, metallic ingénue, compulsive indexer, and co-founder of the Witching Metal band, Hekseri. She has previously published nonfiction and reviews in *Harvard Review*, *The Boston Phoenix*, and *Maelstrom*. "Imperator—Terror Lizard" is her published fiction debut. Stay tuned as the carnage continues with "Imperatrix—Terror Hawk."

Imperator—Terror Lizard: Anyone who knows and loves the 1981 animated fantasy film *Heavy Metal* as much as I do might also bear in mind that there is only one actual heavy metal song in the soundtrack—"The Mob Rules," by Black Sabbath. I love Ozzy, but Ronnie James Dio (1942-2010) is *my team.*

"*TO THE COUNCIL CHAMBERS!*"

Part of the inspiration for "Terror Lizard" comes from that opening scene in Taarna's sequence whereby a mutated strain of exiles invade the city that had shut them out and they fuck it up with excessive enthusiasm and talent. The scene takes only about minute of screen time. But it's a very tasty minute.

In my world, evil is *supposed* to triumph at the beginning, in order to make the reversal of justice prevail with more dramatic flair. Admittedly, I often love stories where the bad guys win in the end—if you're in Tim Robbins kind of mood, compare his fate in *Mystic River* with *Arlington Road.*

"Terror Lizard" is not intended not be one of those stories, where the bad guys win at the very end. In the next chapters, evil will inherit a world of hurt, spawned by its own devices, avarice, and its blind, reckless folly (consider Sauron and His Ring—way to self-destruct, jackhole).

Sickness and convalescence are also an obvious theme in this piece. No one needs to feel sick. Our organismic biology may not be perfect Valhalla, but I think we can all look out for each other without prerequisite scene-points. Stand up and be counted.

To paraphrase that uppermost polestar of stage banter, Tom Araya: that's what we're here to do, to help each other out. Be solid, stand up for what's right, help each other out, and stretch the skies in the name of metal.

The song prompt for "Terror Lizard" is "Terror. Death. Worship!" by Impiety—the finest export from Singapore.

JR Hayes is best known for his involvement with the notorious grindcore band, Pig Destroyer, as well as Enemy Soil and Hissing Choir. A Northern Virginia native, JR has worked enough various jobs to fit a Bukowski short, including Zamboni driver, land surveyor, and Tae Kwon Do instructor. When he's not stalking across a stage like a serial killer, JR enjoys reading anything he can get his hands on, swearing in traffic, and doting on his wife, who may or may not have written this bio.

I don't think **Odious** is something that I would normally write, but I think that's what I like so much about it. A fairytale sprinkled with pop culture references and just a dash of senseless violence. I am honored to be included among all these excellent writers, and I would like to thank Kriscinda and Shawn for their invaluable assistance. I would also like to thank the great Telly Savalas for being kind enough to appear in my story. Cheers.

Mathias Jansson is a Swedish art critic and horror poet. He has been published in magazines as *The Horror Zine*, *Dark Eclipse*,

Schlock, and *The Sirens Call*. He has also contributed to over ninety different horror anthologies from publishers as Horrified Press, James Ward Kirk Fiction, Source Point Press, Thirteen Press, etc.

Seven Goats: The Record Single, Side A & Side B are part of continuing project about the fictional metal band Seven Goats, a band that started in Romania in 1982. The members were arrested by the Communist regime 1984 and accused of conspiracy against the state. Shortly after their arrest the members disappeared and have never been seen again. Most of the records were probably destroyed by the secret police. The band had four members: the twins Vlad (bass), Vlod (Guitar), Lilith (vocal) ,and "One" (drums). The myth says that Lilith was a priestess of an ancient secret cult called "Seven Goats" (from which the band took its name).

Dustin LaValley is an author and screenwriter. His novella from Thunderstorm Books, *The Deceived*, is in pre-production as a feature film. He and his work have been featured in/on PBS, Yahoo News, *Decibel Magazine*, *Fangoria*, *Starburst*, and *3AM Magazine* among others. He's never been in a band, but if you're only into guys who are, then he is that singer for that band.

Isn't Much to Tell: This story is part memoir. Names have been changed while events remain true, until the point of fictionalizing them that is. Perhaps the reason of fictionalizing the ending of a memoir piece was to give myself something exciting to look forward to. Likely not in this case. Anywho . . .

BMX, fighting, Charleston Chew, hardcore, and metal were pretty much it for me and if I somehow entertained you using only those ingredients, then that's not saying much about either of us.

John Edward Lawson has been referred to as "the forgotten black man of horror," but he also regularly publishes literary and science fiction. His novels, short stories, and poetry have garnered nominations for the Dwarf Stars Award, the Elgin Award, Pushcart Prize, Rhysling Award, Stoker Award, and Wonderland Award.

Years of Decay: Frequently the first monster authors summon in their writing is . . . themselves. As somebody with PTSD, I often find myself striking up relationships with others who have the same affliction; we seem drawn to each other. There's a popular notion that people who have been through trauma tend to be more sensitive to suffering in others, but in practice it seems we turn all of our compassion inwards, instead abusing and discarding the people around us arbitrarily. However, it's not enough to recognize this pattern in others. If I'm to maintain any veracity, I have to tackle the "lone survivor in darkness" that manifests within me. So, this is one of those cases where I, as an author, return to that first monster, all while paying homage to one of my favorite albums from the late 1980s.

Shawn Macomber's reportage, essays, and criticism span one decade, five continents, and hundreds of appearances in the pages of a diverse array of publications including *Fangoria*, *Rue Morgue*, *Decibel Magazine*, *Stereogum*, *Magnet*, *Maxim*, *The Wall Street Journal*, *Shock Till You Drop*, *Reason*, and *The Los Angeles Times*, amongst other fine and middling publications. He has covered stories ranging from night raids in the Baghdad suburbs, riots in the Baltics, and two presidential elections to the antics of freedom fighting strip-pole aerobics instructors in rural Pennsylvania, designer cat show devotees at Madison Square Garden, and the Carcass "Exhumed to Consume" reunion tour. His fiction can be found in *Shroud*, *Despumation*, *Fangoria*, and the Grey Matter Press anthology *Savage Beasts*.

Demon Envy: A Romance: As both a devotee of straight-edge hardcore and the lone male reared alongside two sisters by a working single mother, questioning my own sexual impulses and motives proved second nature to me before I really even *had* any legitimate sexual impulses or motives. "The second biggest lie a man tells a woman is, 'The check is in the mail,'" my understandably aggrieved mother would declare as she endured the latest in a seemingly endless trickle of trials, annoyances, and indignities. "The first is, 'I love you.'" That's some heavy shit for a kid dreaming a crazy dream of escaping puberty without becoming an Id-driven male chauvinist sociopath—and I felt an obligation to police myself accordingly. If my fiercely feminine household's worldview presented a conundrum for coming-of-age me, songs like Minor Threat's "Out of Step," Shelter's "Progressive Man," and, later, Earth Crisis' "The Discipline" offered an answer which echoed the straight-edge line on substance abuse, yet nevertheless felt even more radical applied to sex: control myself, reject the *faux* rebellions that are basically training wheels for the most mainstream (mis)behaviors imaginable in western society, and it might be possible to transcend the chaos and addiction I felt predestined to soon inhabit. There is a pre-hardcore precedent for this, incidentally: In *Civilization and Its Discontents* (1930) Sigmund Freud wrote, "[I]t is impossible to overlook the extent to which civilization is built up upon a renunciation of instinct." Like a lot of ideas in that treatise, I believed this before I read it, even if I ultimately prefer the world historic badassery of Karl Buechner yelping "Enslaved by concupiscence, promiscuity leads to despair" at rooms full of sweaty young men *very* in touch with their aggro side. This might seem a weirdly overcooked note for a story as goofy as "Demon Envy," but that *The-Omen*-if-the-kid-were-a-anthropomorphized-cock-monster tale really is a kind of magnified, fantastical engagement of carnality gone bad by an aging dude with a not-embarrassed-by-it-at-all Shelter tattoo whose attraction to straight edge was, despite stumbling into the scene at a moment when militant elements were on the rise, less about playing gangster with a bunch of other white kids at the bottom rung of the lower middle class than embracing a modern day asceticism that might provide an avenue of escape. And I'm still fucking thankful for it too. XOXO.

Wayne Massey is a NYC-born, 17-year Pittsburgh resident who's been shuttering the world around him since high school. When he's not drumming for 'Burgh heavy-doomsters, Molasses Barge, he's listening to music, watching B flicks, and reading.

John Palisano has had articles published in *Fangoria*, *Dark Discoveries* and more. His latest novel *Dust of the Dead* is forthcoming from Samhain, and he's had over thirty short stories published in various markets, two of which were nominated for the Bram Stoker Award. You can reach him at: www.johnpalisano.wordpress.com or facebook.com/johnpalisano or Twitter @johnpalisano.

The Show Must Go On: I grew up going to many metal shows at the long lost New Haven Coliseum. The memories are vivid. I did my best to capture the feeling and language of that period. Yeah. I know. Not as PC as we are these days. But I also wanted to capture the excitement and showmanship of the bands and the audience. Sometimes they were as fun to watch as the musicians. There was a call, which I missed, about doing a period zombie story. That's where this idea came from. What if a zombie infection started at a metal show? Who would know? What if it came and was isolated before word got out? Would anyone know? Or care? I thought it was creepy. I saw some crazy stuff at those shows, and thought it'd be a lot of fun for that reason, and to revisit one of the better concerts I've seen. You can still see the New Haven Coliseum in the Van Halen 'Live Without A Net' concert film. And way up in the back row? One of those little pixels up there was me. Zombies weren't included.

Dutch Pearce is a student at the University of Pittsburgh, a janitor at Whole Foods, and a regular contributor to Decibel Magazine. His fiction has appeared in Thumbnail, a flash fiction journal, as well as on his own blogs, Band of the Week (US),

Dower of Refuse, and Mort Montagne Construction, INC. He also performs vocals and writes lyrics for the ritualistic death metal band, Taphos Nomos. Besides all that, he seldom leaves his room, which he calls The Fortress of Metal.

Summersault was written under the influence of Metallica's *Ride the Lightning*, an album I've been jamming since I was about the same age as the kids in the story. The idea for "Summersault" first came to me when I saw a poster offering $300 for a missing dog. That's a nice score, I thought, and the story just sort of came together from there. Thanks to Scott Koerber for reading every draft I showed him and, through his own excitement, keeping me enthusiastic throughout the revision process.

Jessica Pimentel is popularly recognized as Maria Ruiz on the SAG-award-winning *Orange is the New Black*. She is also the vocalist and recording guitarist for the metal band Alekhine's Gun and bass player for the heavy metal/hardcore band Desolate. Additionally, she is a student of theology and Tibetan Buddhist philosophy, logic, and debate in the Gelugpa Tradition of the Dalai Lama. She was born and raised in Brooklyn, NY.

Lamey Neljor is Tibetan for Guru Yoga. Guru Yoga is a mental and verbal practice used to establish a connection with and merge one's midstream with ultimate wisdom, and bestow the practitioner with a deep sense of mental peace and clarity, purification and healing of body and mind, and a means of gaining merit. This piece is based loosely on the great poem Ganden HlaGyama (A Thousand Angels of the Heaven of

Bliss) tied to the Gelugpa Lineage of Tibetan Buddhism A Prayer of Devotion to Je Tsongkhapa who embodies the bodhisattvas of Compassion (Avalokiteshvara), Wisdom (Manjushri) and Wrathful Power (Vajrapani). Many blessings and prayers are hidden in this work as well as the holy names of the embodiment of compassion, wisdom, and power. Also, because this is dedicated to specific people, their names are intertwined in the poem. It should be read aloud, if possible, and visualized in the first person. The reader/speaker should visualize that this is actually happening to them to the best of their ability. May all beings be free from samsara's ocean of suffering and the causes of suffering. May there always be a lamp on your path. May you become the keeper of the diamond.

Brian Serven organizes words into short stories, poems, and lyrics with a bend toward exploring the human condition and its darker tendencies. He writes music and lyrics for BACKSTABBERS INC., an unrelenting metal- and punk-influenced hardcore band whose most recent album, *M.I.A.*, was released in 2014. When he is not writing and exploring soundscapes, he devotes himself to the martial arts and teaches yoga philosophy.

The Logic of Madness explores the influence a single thought can have on the unraveling of an individual's life. Interwoven among seemingly rational thoughts and notions are perversions and ill-fated literal actions that cause its characters to question and challenge life itself. What is that line we shouldn't cross? Have you already crossed it?

Stephanie M. Wytovich is the Poetry Editor for Raw Dog Screaming Press, a book reviewer for *Nameless Magazine*, and a well-known coffee addict. She is a member of the Science Fiction Poetry Association, an active member of the Horror Writers Association, and a graduate of Seton Hill University's MFA program for Writing Popular Fiction. Her poetry collections, *Hysteria: A Collection of Madness* and *Mourning Jewelry*, can be found at www.rawdogscreaming.com, and her debut novel, *The Eighth*, will be out in early 2016 from Dark Regions Press. Follow Wytovich at stephaniewytovich.blogspot.com and on twitter @ JustAfterSunset.

What I Learned as a Groupie is a piece about repetition, life on the road, and all the sex, drugs, and rock n' roll that goes along with it. At the heart of the piece, it represents the narcissistic gene of an artist, who while engaging in other relationships, is married to his art first and foremost.

32359559R00120

Made in the USA
Middletown, DE
01 June 2016